Blue Tide

Nike Augustine
Book Three
By M.L. Bullock

Yes, 'twas Minerva's self; but ah! how changed,
Since o'er the Darman field in arms she ranged!
Not such as erst, by her divine command,
Her form appeared from Phidias' plastic hand:
Gone were the terrors of her awful brow,
Her idle aegis bore no Gorgon now;
Her helm was dinted, and the broken lance
Seem'd weak and shaftless e'en to mortal glance;
The olive branch, which still she deign'd to clasp,
Shrunk from her touch, and wither'd in her grasp;
And, ah! though still the brightest of the sky,
Celestial tears bedimm'd her large blue eye:
Round the rent casque her owlet circled slow,
And mourn'd his mistress with a shriek of woe!

The Curse of Minerva
Lord Byron, George Gordon (1811)

Chapter One—Nike

Unusual Swim

I didn't have a bucket list—I was a siren and nearly immortal. When would I need one? But I returned to Dauphin Island from vacation feeling as if I had experienced something unique, something I always wanted to do. I probably wouldn't do it again, not for a few hundred years, anyway. But the excursion proved I was free. Free from service as the gate's guardian and free to do as I wished, to some degree. No, bucket lists were really for humans whose lives were like blips on a radar screen, bright and pulsating one second and completely gone from sight the next. Yet taking a vacation was a luxury I'd been wanting to try.

I sailed over the bridge in the rental convertible, the wind whipping my long brown hair around me, Springer sitting beside me in his dog seat belt. His pink tongue hung out, and he looked happy to be returning home. No, it was more than a look. Somehow I *knew* he was happy. I still couldn't figure out how he was here. I thought perhaps he was a figment of my imagination, but everyone saw him, including Cruise and Ramara.

Cruise and Ramara. Yeah, I'd have to figure all that out. I crossed the highest point on the bridge and shivered. So many suicides from this spot. And a few murders. We sailed down the smooth road another half mile and rolled on to Cadillac Avenue. "Almost home now," I said, smiling at Springer as his fuzzy face studied me. Then I caught the blue lights in the rearview mirror.

"Are you kidding me?" I slid back my oversized sunglasses and pulled over beside the bayside marina. This had better not be Kendra Tragic. I wasn't in the mood for any bull. To my surprise, Cruise got out of the car. He straightened his hat and walked toward me. I studied his walk; it was more like an awkward shamble now. He still hadn't completely gotten over his encounter with the vamps a few months ago. Twisted his ankle pretty good. Still, it hadn't slowed him down much.

I put the car in park and turned down Def Leppard. It was October and virtually dead on the island, but that was no excuse for pulling me over. I wanted to chew him out but waited to see what he wanted first.

"Welcome back, Thessalonike."

"You've always called me Nik. What's changed?"

"I like saying it. It's a pretty name." He grinned and leaned down to speak to me face to face.

"Um, thanks. Did you pull me over to tell me I had a pretty name?"

"No, I just wanted to be the first to welcome you back. I missed you. Did you have fun? Where did you go? New Orleans? Pensacola?"

I didn't know how to feel about this conversation, happy that he wanted to see me or ticked off because he pulled me over. A few familiar faces were driving by now. Well, they'd have something to talk about for a while. And what about Kendra Tragic? Didn't it make sense that a shifter would want to hook up with one of his own kind? I decided to give patience a try.

"Yes, I had fun. No, I didn't go to either of those places. May I go home now? Springer needs a bath, and I really want to see what shape my house is in. I left Heliope there alone."

He looked hurt but didn't argue with me. "Sure, but first let me write you this ticket."

"Ticket?"

"Yeah, you were doing 50 in a 35. Watch your speed coming off the bridge there, Speedy." He wrote on his pad while I stared at him incredulously. He ripped off the ticket, folded it in half and handed it to me. "So that's your first ticket, I would imagine. Don't worry. I'm sure the court won't throw the book at you since you're a new driver. I'd ask to see your driver's license, but I'm afraid to know the answer to that question."

Furiously I dug in my purse and pulled out the photo ID. "For your information, Cruise Castille, I do have a license. I insist you write it down!"

He took the license, stared at it and jotted the number on the ticket before handing it back to me. "Have a nice day, ma'am."

I didn't say another word and turned out of the gravel driveway, kicking up rocks before taking off down Cadillac. "What a jerk!" I told Springer. "And to think, I was ready to...well, you know...with him."

I drove down Chaumont, made the curve and saw my house was still standing. There were no gaping holes where the kitchen used to be. No gypsy caravans on the front lawn, no drunken gods passed out in the garden. I pulled the car into the tiny driveway. Maybe I'd buy this car, or one like it. I had some savings left from Jack. Having a car proved to be pretty handy, quite freeing and not at all hard to learn. But then again, I hadn't chosen a standard shift like Liliana had.

"Here we are, boy. Let's grab our stuff and see what the inside of the house looks like." I pulled the crumpled ticket out of the console and read it. There was no citation, just a note that read: *I love you, Nik. Welcome home. Call me later.*

I crumpled the note again after staring at it for a few more seconds. Springer watched me, and I talked to him as if he knew exactly what I was saying. "You'll never guess what's on here. He says he loves me. I can't believe he'd do that." I tossed the ticket in my purse and stood in the driveway. Heliope didn't come running out, and the sound of the ocean commanded my attention. I'd been gone only a week, but that had been such a long time. I wanted to swim. Not think about Cruise's declaration or Ramara's lack of communication. As if he read my mind, Springer bounced off the seat and ran to the shore, barking excitedly.

With a smile, I ran after him and jumped in the ocean completely clothed, minus my glasses and sandals. To my surprise, Springer swam with me, only not as deep or as far from the shore. He splashed along, doing his best to keep up with me. After about fifteen minutes of pure frolicking, I bobbed up next to him. "I'm going to the Down Deep for a few minutes. Don't worry about me. Stay near the shore, okay?" He whimpered unhappily, and I smooched his wet head. "That's the way it's going to be, boy. Wait on the shore for me." He splashed away from me, paddling to the shore with his little dog legs. He'd just have to understand—I needed this. I needed to sing.

In recent days I'd been thinking of a new song. Or maybe it was an old song that I was just now recalling. I couldn't tell anymore. As I swam down, down, down, I hummed the tune. The notes climbed and sank as I lazily pushed myself forward. The water swirled over me, and I reveled in the sensation of being lost in the vastness of it all. A school of blue angelfish zipped past me; their bright yellow and blue colors shone in harmony as they made every move together. It was a beautiful sight. I never grew tired of spotting these gentle fish. Then the peacefulness of the moment passed and my sense of danger awakened. Somewhere just beyond my sight, a predator watched, maybe a shark of some type. Sharks typically ignored me, but this one was curious. Its sonar touched me as it assessed what I was. I wasn't too concerned at the moment, merely aware.

I swam as deep as I wanted to go, yet there was much more of the ocean beneath my feet. It was dangerous to go much deeper alone—that seemed especially true today. And I felt the danger more acutely now; it hovered right at the edge of the artificial reef, waiting. Watching me.

Probably the shark from a moment ago, I reasoned as the water turned icy cold. For humans, it was late in the season for swimming, but my siren blood kept me warm. My special ability was being challenged by an influx of freezing water. I tried to outswim the cold current, paddling faster now, no longer easing through the water. I headed back toward the shore, but whatever followed me seemed fixed on me. Its sonar didn't disconnect from me. By its behavior, I could tell it had decided I was the appropriate target. The school of angelfish puffed past me, and then I had an idea. I accelerated and swam beside them, using them as a barrier against whatever followed me.

What the heck was this? No. Not a shark, but familiar.

Then I felt the first wave. A wave of hate rolled over me and slowed me down. I barely had time to think about it before another wave crashed over me. This one was stronger than the first and nearly took my breath away. Regaining my senses I began to swim, albeit slower than I normally would. The creature's hatred weakened me, made me sluggish.

I can't stay here. I can't wait!

With all my might I kicked my way to the surface, allowing my body to rise like a top. Springer barked wildly on the beach, and I raised my arms to swim to him.

As I made for the beach, the creature slowed its track and I felt the sonar cease. I dipped back under the surface and looked around me. I had to know what it was that stalked me so boldly. I saw a few fish that, like me, fled from the current of cold water. I turned my attention back to the shore, but not before I saw something out of the corner of my eye.

A large tail, green and shimmery, flicked once and disappeared into the depths just beyond the drop-off.

A mermaid's tail.

Chapter Two—Heliope

ove Potion

L I heard the car pull up, but I was glad Thessalonike didn't come racing in the house. How embarrassing that would have been! Smoke billowed out of the oven, and I'd forgotten all about the rice I'd put in the pot on the stove. This wasn't how my first attempt at a family dinner was supposed to turn out. I missed the days when you summoned a servant and requested a tray. Maybe we could do that? Find a cook or a housekeeper? No, that would not satisfy my need to create something—this was a new development in existence. Imagine, after all this time, I'd finally become domestic. Or reasonably so.

The girl had been gone for a week, and during that time I'd fallen in love with the cooking channels. So many exotic dishes to prepare, and the human chefs made it look so easy. If they could do it, why couldn't a newly widowed goddess? Like a student, I'd taken notes, picked out a few recipes, purchased the ingredients and gone to work. My first attempts were okay, but how hard was it to make a grilled cheese and some spinach dip? I realized now that I might have bitten off more than I could chew with my recipe selection.

A failure as a wife, and now a failure at this, I thought as the fire alarm screeched. Angry at myself and everyone else, I smacked it with a broom handle until the plastic machine broke and fell on the floor.

I sniffed at the thought of Agrios, but I was over the foolish old thing. I had to be, didn't I? He'd made his bed, now he could lie in it. For all eternity. Even as I thought the words, I knew I didn't completely feel that way. He'd tried to give me an island, for goodness' sake. He wanted to make me a queen again, but as usual, he did everything wrong. And by his actions he had proved that all he really cared about was himself. Always a selfish being—we were so much alike. Despite all the evil he'd done, cooperating with those vampires, trying to gift Thessalonike and the eloi to Vega in exchange for Dauphin Island, I loved him. His sins didn't kill that love, and it didn't stop me from visiting his resting place every day, but the Order had spoken. My husband would never rise again.

Oh well. On to other things.

I frowned at the blackened beef Wellington and the scorched rice. *I don't think even magic could save this.* I tossed the burnt pan on the stove and ran to open the kitchen windows. As the smoke cleared, I peered out the window over the sink. I could see the dog, or whatever it was, on the beach barking at the water. No doubt it was an enchanted, albeit benevolent, creature. The girl must have gone for a swim. Who could blame her? She'd been plotted against twice now. She must have felt as if she had a virtual and perpetual bull's-eye pinned to her back. Well, I'd stick by her no matter what. She was the last of my family, the last connection I had to humanity and who I had been before. I would not let her down. Not this time.

Except for dinner.

This dinner wasn't going to happen. *Oh well, I tried.* I thumbed through the many restaurant menus that the plastic penguin held in its beak. What a weird ornament for a house. I sometimes wondered about Thessalonike's taste in decorating. It took a while, but I finally found a place that delivered. Not too many island restaurants open this late in the year. I called Voyager's and placed an order for two big baskets of french fries. That was her hands-down favorite. I also ordered a half dozen chili dogs, two root beers and two ice cream cones.

If my attempt at dinner didn't bring a smile to her face, well, maybe the small changes I'd made at the shop would. Business was picking up, thanks to my ingenious idea. I smiled at myself as I began trying to hide the evidence of my failed buffet. Unless she swam for a few hours, there would be no way to hide this stinky disaster.

The dog continued to bark in the distance. I raced around the kitchen, wiping down counters and washing dishes; finally I shoved the pans in the oven and closed the door to hide them. This time I remembered to turn the appliance off. Ransacking Thessalonike's cleaning supplies, I found some scented spray and doused the kitchen with it until I could almost pretend I didn't smell the burnt food. I returned the half-empty can to the basket under the sink and then went to tidy my hair when the doorbell rang. I had gone for a modern hairdo yesterday, a sling-cut bob with feathered bangs. I couldn't resist looking at it every time I passed a mirror.

The doorbell rang again. Geesh, that was fast. I dug in my pocket for some cash. I liked keeping cash on me. It was a modern vice I'd recently discovered. Maybe one day I'd get one of those credit cards. Then I could buy anything I wanted, whenever I wanted. I greedily began plotting how I could fill up the cabinets with nonstick skillets and interesting griddles that left cartoon characters on charred meats—and pancakes! Whatever those were. They looked delicious on television. Maybe I'd try that this weekend.

I opened the door with my money in hand, but there wasn't a soul there. A bouquet of pink roses wrapped in a large piece of pink tissue paper lay on the concrete porch. I rolled my eyes. I wonder which one it was—the cop or the angel? Surely not Ramara. He had too much pride to show up with flowers. I picked them up, brought them inside and plopped them on the kitchen table. A small white card fell out, and strangely enough that wasn't Thessalonike's name on it. It was mine.

What the...? I picked up the neat envelope and rubbed my finger across my name. I slid the card out and read it aloud:

You are more beautiful than any flower.
Your Secret Admirer.

Torn between feeling flattered and uneasy, I scrambled back to the front door and cast a supernatural eye up and down the street. The only other person I could see was Mrs. Bannister, who was waddling out to her mailbox in her worn pink shift and dirty slippers. I sure wasn't going to ask her if she'd seen a sexy calendar hunk delivering flowers to my door. I'd spoken to the nosy old woman once and vowed to never do that again. She wasn't a nice human. Not at all. In fact, I half wondered—

"Heliope! What have you done to my kitchen?" The girl walked in the back door of the house and dropped her bags on the floor. "Did you start a fire? Was anything burned?"

I slammed the front door and went to face my accuser. "Nice to see you, too, stepdaughter. No, I didn't start a fire. The only thing damaged was a pot. And a pan." I couldn't believe she would interrogate me when I'd done all this for her.

"You're too old to pout," she scolded me.

"Okay, so I admit I made a slight miscalculation on the cooking time, but I've ordered some food. I'll replace the accoutrements as soon as my credit card arrives."

"Credit card? How did you manage...never mind. I'm sure I don't want to know."

I grinned at her. "How does french fries and root beer sound? Phew, you two smell like the ocean. Does this animal have to be in here?" The usually friendly dog growled at me, but he didn't flee out the doggie door as he sometimes did when we were alone. I guessed he felt emboldened to show a modicum of bravery with his master so close by.

"Yeah, you're right. We'll go get cleaned up. Thanks for ordering the fries. I hadn't even thought of dinner. I appreciate the effort. It's nice to come home to someone."

She kissed my cheek as she skipped off down the hall, and I just blinked after her. She left her bags near the laundry room door. I wondered if I was expected to do laundry now that I was a widowed goddess with not much power and no prospects whatsoever. Except a dying bouquet of cheap roses.

She poked her head back around the corner. "Please don't touch my laundry." She smiled, and I breathed a sigh of relief. I'd never figure that out. I usually wore supe garments. The "no wash, summon what you want to wear" kind. I didn't know why she didn't do the same. While she argued with the dog about taking a bath, I put the flowers in water and set them on the nightstand in my bedroom. I'd silently taken over Jack Augustine's room and quietly evicted his spirit. It was a room that had a touch of sadness to it, with cool shadows and a comfortable bed. Hopefully Thessalonike wouldn't peek under the bed. I'd never be able to explain what I'd stashed under there.

I flipped on the cooking channel, scowling at that lying Bobby Flay who insisted that "anyone" could whip up one of his trademarked southwestern sauces. Was it true? The last fellow who suggested the beef hadn't been honest at all.

It clearly wasn't a foolproof recipe. I, the great Heliope, was no fool.

By the time the next television program rolled around, the food had arrived. As if by magic, so did Thessalonike and Springer. I shoved the tray of ice cream cones in the freezer and made us a picnic at the living room coffee table. "None for you, dog. You've got a bowl in the kitchen." He groaned and headed off to eat his dinner by himself.

Thessalonike sat on the floor and thanked me again for dinner. "Are you really watching this?" She chuckled as she opened a hot dog and popped a straw into her root beer.

"It's fascinating. Although I admit I'm a bit of an amateur."

In between fries she said, "Just takes some practice. I can't believe you're even trying. That's a huge development." Thankfully she didn't ask why. "How are things at the shop? Probably pretty dead now. Were there any sales this past week?"

"Oh, I forgot. Let me get the numbers for you." I wiped chili off my chin with a paper napkin and went to the refrigerator door. I kept the daily sales numbers on a piece of paper under the Coca-Cola magnet. I had to admit, I was pretty proud of myself. Maybe I wasn't Martha Stewart, but apparently I was a top-notch saleswoman.

"Here you go." I handed the paper to her and got to work on my second chili dog. I felt no shame.

"Heliope, this can't be right." She frowned and squirted more ketchup on her fries. Muting the television, she tapped on the paper. "You mean hundreds, not thousands. See, the point goes here."

I felt my anger rise exponentially. "I may not know how to cook a beef Wellington, but I do know how to calculate wealth. Even here in the New World."

She wiped her hands and tapped on the paper again. "Are you serious? How did this happen? Oh God, you didn't sell the store, did you?"

"What? I'm not an idiot, young lady. I merely added to the stock." I unmuted the television and finished my dinner. "A few Heliope specialties." Retrieving the remote control from the wooden coffee table, she pressed the mute button again.

"What do you mean? Please tell me you haven't been casting spells or working magic. You'll have the Order breathing down our necks, Heliope."

"No, no. Nothing like that. Well, maybe kind of like that. I did create some cool potions, and they are selling like hotcakes. Which reminds me, do you have a pancake griddle?"

She shoved a wisp of brown hair behind her ear and stared at me. "What kind of potions?"

"Just some harmless love potions. Mostly red Kool-Aid and a few other spices, but it gets the job done well enough. I have a whole line of love potions. Some for falling in love, some for rekindling the romance, some for repelling a boss or an ex. Can't believe how many people need romantic help."

"I don't think I'm licensed to dispense love potions, Heliope. Just souvenirs."

"Well, that sucks. I've got another batch of 'Kiss Me' potion brewing in the storeroom."

"It's not explosive, is it?" She got up on her knees, ready to run to the shop.

"Stop acting like I'm a schoolgirl. Of course it's not. I don't blow up things...intentionally. Will you please trust me for once? I got tired of nobody coming in the shop. If the tourists are gone, you'll need to market to the locals. The supes have been flocking, and more than a few humans. I thought I was helping." This was certainly not the response I'd expected.

"I'm sorry. I'm just not used to anyone helping me in the shop. It's been just me for a long time. If these numbers are accurate, which I'm sure they must be," she added quickly, "then you've really pulled out a miracle here. You might have just saved Shipwreck Souvenirs."

I smiled, uncaring if I had cheese in my teeth. It felt good to do something right for a change. I'd made so many mistakes...my whole life felt like a mistake at times.

Success! So this was what modern success felt like. It was a good feeling—no wonder everyone wanted it. I'd enjoy the feeling of accomplishment for now and tell her about the thing under my bed later. No sense in getting into a fight right now. The new episode of *Cook My Tail Off* was coming on, and the commercial promised an "epic shrimp battle."

And there was ice cream.

Chapter Three—Cruise

Tidal Wave

"You ever watch ThunderCats growing up?" I asked Deputy Tragic as we sat in the squad car with binoculars focused on the boat. We were waiting to see if Earl dumped his illegal fish into the marina or if he sold them direct to a buyer. He'd been waiting around for a while, looking nervous. I knew he had the fish; his ex-deckhand had called to rat on him. I had hoped it wasn't true, though. I hated coming down on fishermen—they were like cops and firemen to me. They were the good guys who kept everything going. At least most of them. This kind of bust wasn't good for business, but the mayor had a bug up his butt about this new federal law. From what I gathered, the old saying was true: "Crap always rolls downhill." I didn't understand the need for all the rules and regulations they forced these guys to comply with. Especially red snapper fishermen like Earl. But I was just a dumb hick with a badge. I imagined if I asked Kendra, she'd agree wholeheartedly with that assessment.

She looked at me like I was stupid. "What? Is that supposed to be a joke?"

"ThunderCats? The cartoon? You've never heard of it?"

"No, I haven't. Sounds stupid." She squinted into the binoculars, the iciness in her voice more than apparent. Even to someone as dense as me. I didn't understand her. She went from wanting to be my shifter mentor to being absolutely no help at all. And that was after I saved her life!

Thankfully, Vern, her dad, came around every couple of days and answered my questions. I had to admit some of them were pretty stupid, but I had no idea what being a shifter meant. My own father had been gone quite a while. Couldn't ask him anything about Mom and what I saw. He just took off one day, telling me a lie about having to pick up some new rods and tackle. I guess he'd had enough of my dumb questions too.

"You want to tell me what you're pissed about? I mean, even if you don't want to be friends, we do have to work together. Can't we do our jobs without all the secret conversation? It's been months."

"Secret conversation?" She sounded even more exasperated now.

"Yeah, you know what I mean. The conversations you have in your head, the ones you think people don't hear?"

"Are you a mind reader?" Her eyes widened at the thought that I might know what she was thinking about.

"Not exactly, but I ain't stupid. I know you're hating on me. Let's go ahead and clear the air. Just give it to me straight, Kendra." I dropped the "Officer" since I was talking to her as a friend.

"All right then, jerk-face. I'm lying on the floor in that bunker, and you're arguing with the eloi about who's going to get stuck taking me to safety. Did you even think how I'd feel about that? I'm always second! However you feel about her, I'm the one lying on the floor bleeding to death. What the hell, Cruise? Even if you only think of me as a friend, that was pretty ridiculous."

I tried not to laugh in her pretty face. Her blond ponytail with the curl at the end bounced as she enunciated her last few words dramatically. She was clearly in the right here. I had acted like a jerk that day, but then again it had been my first time going "mano a mano" with a vampire. Couldn't she cut me some slack? I mean, I had saved her life.

"Well? What do you have to say for yourself, buddy?"

Before I could drum up a witty comeback, the radio squawked to life. Our new dispatcher and secretary, Regina Fields, talked in a rush. "Chief? Deputy Tragic? Where y'all at? Answer me back, over!"

Kendra and I reached for the radio at the same time. I bumped her hand, and she pulled back as if I were too toxic to touch. Our talk obviously hadn't done any good.

"We're here. Down by the East End Marina. What's up?"

"Get out of there, Chief! Get back to the station now! Tidal wave is coming!"

Before I could ask another question, I heard the island sirens going off from the courthouse and the schoolhouse. "What the hell is going on? Who turned on the tornado siren? What tidal wave?"

"Um, move the car! Now, now!" Kendra lurched in her seat and pointed out into the Gulf. A massive wave was coming this way, the kind of rogue wave that sometimes showed up when a hurricane or tropical storm was approaching. I hadn't gotten any bulletins about bad weather, but it was definitely coming. I swung the car around and paused. "What about Earl? We can't leave him here."

"He's on a boat. He'll have to ride it out, Cruise! Get going now or we're dead! Unless you can shift into a shark! I sure as hell can't!"

I drove like a lunatic toward the station. We crossed onto Cadillac just as the wave slapped the southern shore of the island. It was an eerie sight. There were no dark clouds, not even a small puff of white in the sky—just a six-foot wall of water crashing against the land. Water sloshed under the car but didn't get in. I didn't know how I'd explain requisitioning another squad car so soon after getting this one. Kendra and I pulled into the police station and waited for the water to stop sloshing. The police station's platform had thankfully kept the floors dry. Regina met us at the door.

"Thanks be! I am so glad to see you two alive. It's a disaster of the first order!" Regina had an unusual accent; I assumed she was Irish, but sometimes she dove off into something not quite Irish. She was a kind if overly excitable person. That was kind of unfortunate, considering she was an emergency dispatcher. We'd gotten lots of calls about some first-order disaster that turned out to be a minor infraction or a prank call. Still, she took her job seriously, and I couldn't afford to be picky. She was my third dispatcher.

"Scientists from the USGS are on the way. The mayor is on the phone, and I'm getting a bunch of calls from people needing help, Chief," Regina blurted out in a rush as she met us at the door. All the phones were ringing, and I rubbed my stubbled face.

Breathe, Castille. You can do this.

"Tell the mayor he'll have to wait. Let's call someone in to help us with the phones, Regina. What about Roger over at the service station? He's always willing to help, and he's close by. When the USGS get here, give them what they want. They can use my office if they need to. I have a feeling I'm not going to see it for a while. Then call FEMA and the Red Cross, see if we can get some help down here. Let's set up at the school, just like during a storm."

"Okay, Chief." She ran back to her desk and jotted down some notes. If nothing else, Regina was grade-A at taking notes.

"And I need to know if this is an isolated incident or if we should expect more," I called after her as she raised her hand while talking to herself. I turned to Kendra and said, "Grab the extra emergency kit. I'll grab the walkie-talkies; we'll use those to stay in touch. Let's recon the East End so we can figure out what areas are most affected. Hopefully it's just this one side. Fewer homes over here."

"Yeah, but a lot more boats," she said, sliding on her slicker. I did the same and grabbed my keys off my desk. We grabbed the supplies and bolted out the door.

As we walked out, Roger jogged across Cadillac. "I'm here, Chief. Regina says you need help."

Kendra cranked the car. I could see she wanted to be in control, and I was okay with that for the moment. I needed eyes on the ground.

"Yeah, can you help her with the phones? Send us priority calls only, okay? And I forgot to tell her, we need to mobilize the fire department."

"I've got you covered, Chief." We peeled out of the parking lot, and all I could do was hang on and stare at the mess the wall of water had left behind. It had been destructive, but it could have been worse. I hoped it didn't get worse. Immediately, I picked up the phone and called Nike. She didn't answer, of course, so I left a voicemail. I felt Kendra stiffen beside me, but I couldn't help that right now.

"Hey, Nik. It's me. Just checking on you. Please let me know you're okay."

I had barely hung up when she called me back. "Cruise, are you okay?" she asked. "What just happened? I heard a loud boom!"

"Tidal wave hit the East End."

Without hesitation she asked, "What can I do?"

"Head to the school. They'll set up an emergency station there. Don't let anyone drink the water. We'll have to check the water supply. We'll need all the bottled water we can find."

"I'm on it."

"Thanks, Nik." I didn't linger on the phone. I had a job to do. Kendra made the turn from Cadillac onto Fort Morgan Road. I couldn't believe what I was seeing. Earl's boat, Dreamsicle, was lying in the middle of the gravel road, and he was on the ground next to it.

Kendra slammed on the brakes, and I bolted from the vehicle to check on the old man. He was breathing, thankfully, but he didn't look too good. "Radio for an ambulance!" I shouted to her. "Come on, Earl. Stay with me!"

His dark eyes, full of pain, flew open at the sound of my voice.

"I'm right here, Earl. Ambulance is on the way. Kendra, bring me a blanket!"

He grabbed my arm and pulled me down to him so I could hear him whisper something.

"What is it, Earl? You need to stay calm. Help is on the way."

He didn't loosen his grip. In a pained voice, he said one word: *Minerva!*

Chapter Four—Nike

Attack Mode

Heliope's "radar" was going off, Springer wouldn't stop barking and I was doing everything I could not to freak out. The ground had stopped shaking now; Heliope and I had thought it was an earthquake at first, because what else could it have been? At least Cruise was okay. From the first reports on the local radio station, the tidal wave was completely unexpected. There was some talk about an offshore earthquake, but those didn't normally occur down here in south Alabama. "Nope, it's supernatural. Definitely." She pursed her lips thoughtfully and "listened" for clues. After a moment she shook her head in exasperation. "It's just not clear." She followed me to the bedroom as I hurriedly dressed.

"What does the Order say?" I asked her as I slid on my worn jeans, a long-sleeved blue t-shirt and a pair of pink rubber boots.

Looking skyward she asked, "Any clues, guys? Anyone watching the gate? Can you see us down here?" I didn't know if she was serious or not, so I looked around the room with her. No scroll appeared. Springer continued to bark, but I refused to unlock the doggie door for him. The last thing I needed was for him to get washed away or lost. I had just gotten him back after several decades. I couldn't lose him again.

"Sorry, boy. You stay home and watch the house. You have my permission to bite any intruders." I absently hoped Ramara would show up at my house unannounced. He used to do that all the time, but I hadn't seen him in weeks. And I couldn't make myself drive over there. He could read my mind, and I didn't want him to know I'd read the scroll. It seemed so wrong now. But how was I to know it had been for him? It's not like the Order addressed the scrolls. I scratched Springer's ears, but he bit the tail of my shirt and wouldn't let go. "No, I have to go. I promised Cruise. You stay with Heliope."

"I'm not staying here. I'm going too." In the blink of an eye she'd changed her clothing. She'd swapped out her gauzy taupe sundress with a trapeze hem for a pair of camouflage pants, a khaki green tank with a matching jacket and shiny black combat boots. To top off the ensemble, she wore a pair of sparkly dangling earrings and some serious eye makeup typically reserved for a model's photo shoot. I didn't know whether to laugh or start rubbing her eyes with my sleeve.

"No way. And why are you dressed like you're about to enlist in the military? Or hit the catwalk."

"This is the trend for emergency situations. Don't you ever watch television? Just wait. You're going to stick out like a sore thumb with those horrible boots on. Pink doesn't go with a blue t-shirt. Let me whip up something for you!" Heliope raised her hand, ready to cast her unique brand of magic. "We can match!"

"No! Please, don't! I'm good, and you look great. I take it all back. Thanks, but are you sure you want to go? I don't know when I'll be back, and I would hate for you to miss your shows." That was a weak attempt at distraction, but it was all I had at the moment.

"Nope, I'm ready and reporting for duty!"

"Oh goodness. Well, okay. Springer, stay out of trouble. I'll be back soon." I had grave misgivings about having her "help" me, but I couldn't make her stay here.

I drove the rental car to the school; it was only a quarter mile, but we needed every second. Emergency services were establishing an early presence, and many islanders were already gathering for first aid assistance. I parked the car out of the way, and Heliope and I helped get things going. Lots of supes had showed up to help, and many of them had that familiar *What the heck is going on?* expression. I didn't have any answers and didn't offer any guesses. My goal was to keep a low profile and help the island's residents. I helped move the stacks of stored water to the gym, gave candy to the kids and set up the registration tables. An hour later and as predicted, Heliope was ready to abandon her post at the table. Children were naturally curious about the fancy lady, but the feeling definitely wasn't mutual. She didn't appreciate their attention or their curiosity. But I did notice that one resident lingered around her quite a bit. His name was Jolly Jeff Treadmire, and he owned the island's first gym, Double Time. Once upon a time, he had probably been a striking man. But time had gotten the best of him, as it always did in the human world. He had a bald head—not by choice—a trim beard and excessive muscles. Some would have considered him handsome, but Heliope treated him with disdain.

And he appeared to like it.

"Why are those small humans staring at me?" she wanted to know as I passed by with a box of crayons and coloring books.

"Because you're the prettiest woman here. Now smile and act like a human."

She made a *pfft* sound and whispered back, "That's not helpful. I thought I *was* acting like a human."

"Act like a *kind* human."

"I want extra for character work," she growled as another youngster came by to borrow one of her pens. Treadmire intervened and led the kid to another table.

Fortunately for us, fewer than a hundred people needed our assistance with water and shelter. Everything was under control now, and I was ready to check on Springer. There were reports of serious damage to the businesses and the few homes on that end of the island, but it looked like it could have been much worse. That was something to be thankful for.

"Let me go tell Jolly we're stepping out for a minute. Then I'll take you home."

"I'm so exhausted," she said dramatically. "You won't be long, will you? Hey, bring that pen back, you little..."

"Heliope!"

"I mean, please bring that back soon, dear." She waved to a curious parent and crossed her eyes at me in protest from behind her rickety fold-up table.

"Oh no. What's he doing here?"

I looked in the direction she was pointing. It was Ramara, soaking wet and looking like he'd been dragged out of the ocean. And never sexier.

Oh no! Shields up! Shields up! I reminded myself. *Please don't read my mind,* I said to myself, half hoping that he'd hear me.

To my surprise, he nodded once and gave me a glum look. "Are you busy? I need your help on the boat."

Heliope about jumped over the table to join us. "I'm in. What are we looking for?"

"Missing college kid. She's my neighbor's daughter. Everyone else is accounted for. She was near the beach when the wave hit. She's a pretty good swimmer, so it's possible she's hanging on somewhere."

"Sure, I'll be glad to help. Let me tell Jolly we're leaving." Five minutes later Heliope and I were in the convertible wheeling our way to The Outcast. Ramara beat us there, of course, and he was ready to go. I climbed on board, but Heliope hesitated.

"I can't go."

"What is it?" I asked, pausing on the pier. Surely she wasn't going to waste valuable rescue time being dramatic. I'd choke her if she acted a fool.

"I can't go, and I can't explain. You two go. Be safe." She had a weird expression on her face, as if she might go into a trance or something. Ramara's anxiety was like a living thing, and I didn't have time to argue.

"Okay? Got your house key?"

"Yes, right here." She patted her bra as she looked at something I couldn't see. I didn't ask any more questions.

"All right, see you at home. You sure you're okay?"

"Yep, never better. Be careful." With that she turned and walked back to the marina, and I watched her disappear as the boat eased out.

I hoped it wasn't the last time I saw her. I couldn't handle too many more last times.

Chapter Five—Heliope

War Drums

      I waited for the boat to leave the marina before I took to the water. In a flash I changed my garments to something more majestic. I looked up and down the beach, but there was no one around. The supes would be on the other side of the island now, rescuing the stranded and securing the homes and boats. It was all very human, but this was our home too.

I heard it again.

Thump. One loud bang and two short ones. *Thump-thump.*

Technically, I was of the Oceanid order, minus the diving skills of a siren or mermaid. I stood on the ocean floor, the water murky and dark with silt around me. Of course it would be after a tidal wave. A moving of the waters at such force was bound to stir up the silt and maybe a few other things. Luckily for the islanders here, on a scale from one to ten, today's wave was maybe a two or three. The people of Dauphin Island hadn't seen destruction like I'd seen in centuries past—but others had.

One wave in the Pacific Islands had such strength it washed the entire main island away. Another time the entire coastline of Greece rocked and reeled like a drunkard before resettling with much loss of life and property. Both of those times, tidal waves had meant only one thing—a war under the waters.

I kept my eyes open and waited for the sound to come closer.

Thump. Thump-thump.

It would be better to speak first. I whispered into the void of water, "I am Heliope. Why are you here?"

I didn't bother putting up a defense, and showing fear so soon in a potential skirmish would be foolish. Besides, I'd come here for a purpose. I wanted to get to the bottom of this sound, and I wasn't going to run away like a coward. The thumping irritated me to the core and stirred up something else I wasn't accustomed to—fear.

Thump. Thump-thump.

The source of the sound approached me. It—no, she—knew I was here, and there was no turning back. She swam about me in a wide perimeter just out of my line of sight. When she was ready to reveal herself to me, she let out a crushing wail of anger and pain and came at me like a bullet.

Oh yes, this was personal.

The water glowed green and grew colder ahead of her, and it whooshed around me like a living force. I detected there was more than one being approaching me, but there was only one leader. And she was a queen.

Minerva!

I inwardly groaned but kept my face like one of the white stone statues that were chiseled in my honor in ancient times. I wished it were so now, for my statuesque appearance was all a pretense. Even my innards were quivering. Power to power, there was no competition here. This creature was far older and much stronger than I. She had power I could only dream of. Though I'd never laid eyes on her before, I knew this was Minerva, Queen of the Mermaids. Queen of a dying race and mother of Meri. That had to be why she was here.

She wanted her daughter, and I was the last to be seen with her.

Behind Minerva's green glow hovered a retinue of warrior maidens, each with a menacing look of hatred directed at me. Minerva swam in increasingly smaller circles around me until she and I were face to face. Like many of the old supernaturates, she was lovely in an empty, gloomy way. Her long black hair didn't wave about her like her dreamy-eyed daughter Meri's blond locks did. She wore a string of glistening emeralds as a headband that kept her tresses under control like twisted ropes. She was no Gorgon with snakes swimming about her head, but she was equally intimidating. I met her eyes without fear. Minerva's nose was straight, and her full lips were closed and dark. Her skin shimmered slightly, but she kept most of her body clothed in the darkness of the sea. Her most startling feature was her eyes, green with triangular black pupils—two pinpoints completely void of light that bored into my soul without fear of reprisal.

And why should she fear me? The shimmer of mermaids crept closer too, feeling emboldened by their queen. My heart didn't seem to remember that it was immortal. A fraction of humanity remained hidden inside me. I was afraid.

She smiled...and then the smile disappeared. She raised her royal head and looked down at me. The mermaids behind her moved even closer to me. One carried a bit of stretched skin and the others carried weapons, crude bone spears and other things I didn't recognize, but they all looked altogether deadly. She peered down, reminding me who I was and who she was. I took the hint and bowed my head in deference to the stronger being. She pedaled back a foot, then whizzed around me and slapped me once with her glistening green tail. Her strike knocked the wind out of me, and again my humanity—and the fear—kicked in. I tried to swim to the surface; it wasn't far above me, maybe twenty feet, but it might as well have been twenty miles.

Minerva snatched my flowing gown and pulled me back down to the sandy bottom.

Daughter! Mine!

She didn't use words but showed me what she was after—her child, a wayward child who had sinned against her shimmer but was not forgotten.

Without much effort, Meri's face came to mind momentarily, and then Minerva's face appeared in front of me. She waited to hear something. She knew I knew what happened to Meri.

The memory rushed back to me...the battle at the Sirens Gate. The struggle for the necklace and Meri's hiding of Alexander's bones. The brave Meri's protection of Thessalonike and finally my desperate journey through the gate with the mermaid's lifeless body.

I felt again my utter surprise at where the gate had taken us. When the gate opened on the other side, we were standing at the foot of the Stoa of Attalos. This was proof to me that the Order watched and directed me, for here all things were possible. Once this had been a place of healing where the divine met the earth. I walked up the steps with Meri in my arms. My feet slapped against the cold marble, and as I walked closer to the row of statues that waited at the other side I sensed that time was shifting. It was an experience I'd had only twice before, and it shook me to the core. As I drew closer to my destination, an ancient woman stepped out from behind a column, a sacred fan in her hand. And with it she'd waved to the space before the center statue. My eyes cast to the ground; I did not meet Faydra's watchful gaze. I laid the broken mermaid on the marble and stepped back. The woman's dark eyes shifted to a place beyond me, and I left with regret.

A sob escaped me as Minerva pulled the memory from me. Then another memory came unbidden to my mind. My only daughter's face.

Thessalonike! No! She is not responsible—this was Nemesis' doing!

Now the entire shimmer, at least six mermaids, surrounded me. Their glistening tails slapped me as Minerva gave an angry screech. Who would know what happened to me? Was it possible that I could die? I, the great Heliope, drowned in the ocean by ferocious mer-warriors? From somewhere deep inside me, pride burst forth, and with it my strength.

I flung my hands in front of me, moving the green waters back and repelling the furious mermaids. Minerva slipped back but not too far.

It would not take long for her to realize this was only glamor-magic, not a true demonstration of power. Her presence had diminished me somehow. That was another first that I would have to examine later—if I survived. The shimmer moved back behind their warrior-queen. Slowly now she hung before me, her head tilted, those black pupils piercing. She said only four words to my mind. Although she had an odd accent, her voice sounded strong and clear.

My daughter. Your daughter.

And with that she spun away, taking her drums and her warriors with her.

With all my might I swam for shore.

Chapter Six—Nike

R*escue Me*
Ramara yelled at someone on the radio. "You get over there now! I'm working the current toward you. She's got to be here, and we've got to find her before she goes out to sea. Over."

Crackling noise, and then an apologetic voice came over the radio. "We've been at this for hours, Ray. I think you might have to face the fact that she's already out to sea. Over."

"Don't want to hear it. Just do it. Over."

"Fine, working the Frenchman's current—again. Over."

He hung up the radio and ignored the other captain's additional words. He didn't chitchat with me either, and I spent my time looking out on the water with my binoculars. I quietly wondered why he didn't do a flyover and find her himself. Unless for some reason he couldn't fly anymore. I swallowed at that thought. I hoped that wasn't the reason. No, that couldn't be right. It had to be because there were too many human eyes out here on the water right now. I could see the other boat on the other side of the current. Finally when he wouldn't talk at all I said, "How long have you been looking for this girl? Is she someone you know?"

"Not really. I mean, kind of. Her parents live on their boat, just like I do. Their boat is docked next to mine—she was visiting them for the weekend. They were out in the boat when the wave hit. My neighbors are fine, but Emily disappeared. I promised her father I would find her. No matter what."

I raised the binoculars again and scanned the surface. There wasn't much to see. Patches of garbage left over from the washout after the wave and some boats. "You know, searching like this isn't the best method." I hoped he'd get my hint about him flying, but he didn't say a word.

I sighed and told him, "I need to get in the water, Ramara. I bet I could find her in no time." I didn't wait for his answer. I put the binoculars down and began stripping off clothing. I pulled off my rubber boots and slid out of my worn, dirty blue jeans. Thank goodness I hadn't reached for my leopard-print underwear this morning. No need to make this more awkward than it had to be. I pulled off the long-sleeved t-shirt and left on my undershirt, then put my hair in a ponytail and twisted it into a bun. Ramara did not wear his usual smirk; his serious expression was respectful and thoughtful. I found myself wondering what he was thinking. If only I could read his mind. He helped me down the ladder. I could have just dived in, but I liked feeling my hand in his. "Hey," he said in a rough voice.

"Yeah?" I asked him as I slid into the water.

"Thanks for this."

"It's no biggie, Ray." I smiled at him as I used his human name. He was calling me Nik, so I could call him Ray. "Her name is Emily, right?"

"Yeah, that's right. Please find her, Nik."

"I'll be back." I dipped under the water and began searching, singing and searching some more. Finding nothing close to the boat, I swam south, very much aware that both the shore and the boat were disappearing behind me.

Pretty soon a pod of young dolphins trailed me, curious as to why a siren was swimming at breakneck speed through their water. I couldn't communicate with them easily, but they weren't leaving me alone. I touched one as he passed me to show him I was his friend. He and his pod broke left and abandoned me.

Trouble! Trouble and danger!

Come back, I called. *I am not trouble or danger. I'm here to find a human girl.*

Trouble and danger! Flee!

I turned immediately and headed back to the boat. As I surfaced I could see a pile of garbage not far away. Despite whatever trouble and danger the dolphins detected, I had an obligation to check it out. I had promised Ramara, and he had done so much for me. I could not let him down. I heard the boat turning my way and in the direction of the pile of floating junk, some kind of foam siding and household debris. And yes! I did see a human lying on it, facedown and unmoving.

I heard Ramara pointing and calling, "Emily! Emily!" At the same time the dolphins still declared, *Trouble and danger! Trouble and danger!* Then they were gone, and I was left alone in the water. Nothing stirred around me. No stingrays, no blue sharks, no fish. Nothing. And that was worrisome.

I dove under the troubled water. It would be faster to close the distance to the garbage pile if I swam below the surface. Then I heard it: *Thump! Thump-thump!* It was definitely an on-purpose sound, like someone was sending a message, but what? Maybe the human girl was tapping on something, exhausted and trying to get our attention?

No, that couldn't be right. I paused in the water and stared down. There was a green glow deep under me. What the heck was that? I bobbed back up top and heard Ramara yelling at me, "Get back here!" I ignored him. I was too close to the girl on the haphazard stack of foam pieces.

"Hey, Emily! Emily!" I called to her as I got closer.

She lifted her head weakly. "Here. I'm here."

"Ramara!" I yelled, but it was pointless. The boat was plowing swiftly toward us, but so was a wall of green-tinted water. Emily's eyes were wide as she spotted the wave behind me. She let out a scream, and I clambered up next to her on the broken platform. The wave climbed higher and inched closer.

"Hold on to me!" I screamed at her as the water crashed down on us. The force of the water sent us underwater twenty feet, and I felt Emily struggle beside me. I grabbed her arm and sped to the surface. I felt her hand slide out of mine—I could see the flicker of a tail in the crush of water. And it was not the tail of a fish. I dove after Emily, who was unconscious now and slipping into the deep. Since she couldn't hear me, I blasted a few notes of a song to repel the sea creature so I could grab the human and drag her to the surface.

I shoved Emily up and onto her back. The surface sloshed, and the waves threatened to gather again. Ramara was there now beside me, helping me carry Emily's limp body out of the tumultuous water. I heard the thumping again and stared down as I climbed up the ladder. There! I saw the iridescent tail glistening beneath me—a mermaid's tail. And then another. And yet another. As the green glow expanded, the beating of a mystical drum pounded in my head.

Minerva had come, and she had come for me.

Chapter Seven—Heliope

Sacred Stone

S I hid behind a dune waiting for the last of the rescuers to leave the beach area. Once I activated the gate, everyone would see it, including the humans. That was something the Order would never permit. I didn't need as much power as Roxana had required. I didn't have to wait on a star alignment or light from the moon. My only concern was getting back to the Stoa of Attalos. Where would the gate take me this time? This was the last Oceanid gate, and I was pretty convinced that without the Order's intervention the last time, I would never have made it back to Greece.

I glided across the sand and summoned the magic with my hands. With one more quick peek around me, I opened the gate and quickly stepped through it. I had to find Meri and bring her back, or else Minerva would destroy Thessalonike.

My daughter. Your daughter. That was no cryptic message but a promise. Minerva would have justice—her brand of justice. There would be no reasoning with the being. Like all mermaids, Minerva relied upon her emotions to guide her. What she felt, she felt exponentially. At the moment, she felt raging anger.

As the fog cleared, I could see that I was not at the Stoa. Instead I was standing before the white columns of the High Council, the heart of the Order. The meaning of this was also clear. I wasn't going anywhere without their approval. This would mean more red tape, more pleading for help, more time away from my task. I was beginning to hate the politics of it all. I paused in the blue fog and could feel the presence of others near me, but I didn't step toward them. They waited for me, beckoned me.

Without a word I waved my hands again, opened the gate and left the Order behind. I had to continue my search. Thessalonike needed me. I had promised her mother that I would do all I could to protect her only daughter. We had been friends, Niceipolis and I—before Philip entered our lives and plowed that friendship under like the bull of a man that he was, at least for a time. I never loved him, but when Niceipolis perished just three weeks after giving birth to the girl, some say at the hands of her unhappy husband, I stepped into her sandals. Like most women in those days I had little choice in the matter, but I did not fight my fate. It was a privilege to be the wife of the king of Macedonia, who would later become the father of Alexander the Great.

But times were different then. Minotaurs creeped through labyrinths, so-called gods crept into the beds of noble women and magic hung over the world, changing it constantly. And to think, the majority of modern culture shunned such things. They reserved their faith for things they could study under a microscope. Niceipolis had been an exceptionally intelligent woman. While the ancient world celebrated beauties like that brainless twit, Helen of Troy, women like Niceipolis—and myself, dare I say—were shaping governments, influencing leaders.

Niceipolis had a quiet, elegant beauty, but she wasn't one to parade through town draped in jewels, as Philip and most men of the time preferred. Thessalonike was very much like her. She was beautiful but not the kind of beauty that required props. And she was intelligent.

Oh, Niceipolis! I have missed you!

The magic of the gate ceased, and I stepped out again. This time there was no fog swirling. No supernaturates to greet me. Only an empty plain of tall wheat grass. I spun around to return to the gate, but it was gone. Hidden by the Order, no doubt.

"No!" I screamed. "Let me through! I have to find Meri before it is too late!" I waved my hands to try to force the gate to appear, but whoever hid it had greater magic than I. With all the strength I could muster I waved my hands again, but with the same results. I screamed in anger but refused to abandon my mission. There had to be another way, something I could use to compel the gate to open, like a sacred stone. In ancient times, during the time of the Great Quarrels between the races, gates were summarily opened and closed without much notice. Thankfully, magic words recorded on sacred stones could be used to force the gate to work during such "quarrels." *Didn't humans ever wonder where the word "abracadabra" came from?* On a whim, I tried it here. Nothing.

I scanned the horizon. The nearest thing to me was a clump of trees. Perhaps the stone was there. Cedar trees, like the kind that Agrios enjoyed lingering beneath, were old and made good landmarks for old creatures like me. There was nothing else around, only endless fields of tall brown grass. I walked toward the trees, half-expecting something to leap out of the grass. This place had that kind of feeling.

"You'll just have to understand, Faydra. She is my daughter," I said in a whisper, not sure if she heard me. Who was I kidding? Of course she heard me. My disobedience would ensure one thing—that the Order now watched my every move.

I kept my eye on the tree line and thought about Niceipolis. The day she'd thrown her body across the Compendium of Hope when a priest in her household threatened to burn it. The time she'd stood in the amphitheater, a knife at her neck because she wouldn't bow to Philip's horrid oldest daughter, Cleopatra of Epirus. If Philip hadn't intervened, I can't say what would have occurred, but my friend had not cowered in the face of adversity.

And when she died, I could hardly believe it. The birth of Thessalonike had been hard on her, but she'd not stayed in bed long. She was back on her feet caring for Philip and his household with the polished grace of a noblewoman who enjoyed the love of her family and her country. And then she was dead. Found dead. Cold dead in her bed, Philip halfway across the country, making marriage arrangements for the ungrateful Cleopatra. And then he would die soon after.

Only I was left to shield the last remaining issue of the line of Macedon.

As my head swam with memories, I noticed that I had not made much progress. In fact, I was back where I started, according to the path I had tread. I began my trek again, careful to keep my eyes and mind trained on the path ahead of me. Then I felt it, a flicker in the air, evidence that what I was seeing wasn't altogether real. I waved my right hand in an arc, and the scene changed. The fog returned, and the presence of supernaturates became apparent.

I had never left the steps of the Council. With much trepidation, I walked up the stone ramp past the flickering Flames of Truth and into the long hall, the home of the Higher Order.

Time to face the music.

Chapter Eight—Cruise

Cry Wolf

"Mayor Bostwick, can you give us the latest on what's happening here on Dauphin Island?"

Jacketless with rolled-up sleeves, the mayor nodded thoughtfully at the reporter, a young man about my age. He held the microphone in Sherman Bostwick's face, barely looking at him.

The mayor pretended he didn't notice the guy's aloofness. "Thank you, Chris, for covering this very important human story. Contrary to popular belief, we haven't washed away down here, but there is significant damage to the aquarium, the ferry and many other properties on the east end of the island. We haven't lost anyone, which is the most important thing, but we had some near misses. Luckily, our siren system warned us of the danger, and islanders were able to take shelter. I'm sure that's what saved us."

"Those sirens were installed a few months ago, right?" The mayor nodded proudly, and the reporter prodded him a bit more. "How much time passed between the sirens going off and the arrival of the wave, mayor? Half an hour? Fifteen minutes?"

"Chris, from what I understand, the sirens gave us a few valuable minutes, and that's what saved lives here. I will be the first to admit that it wasn't much time, certainly not enough to protect much of the property, but lives were saved. That's all that really matters in the end."

I shook my head off camera, hardly believing what I was hearing. No, we hadn't lost anyone—not yet—but we did have two missing people. I couldn't let this charade continue without speaking up. I was the Chief of Police, for God's sake. These people were my responsibility. I walked up quietly and stood behind the mayor, hoping the reporter would get the hint, and he did exactly that. He thanked the mayor and then acknowledged me on air, finally, after Bostwick blathered on about how the jetties protected the fort and how the USGS had to be wrong about the whole earthquake thing.

"Anything you care to add, Sheriff?"

"Chief, I'm Chief Castille." I held my hat in my hands and gave him a friendly smile. Where was this guy from? I thought every reporter in the area knew that I had taken Belloc's place. Maybe not. Still, if he could help me get the word out about the missing people, I didn't care what he called me.

"Pardon me, Chief. Anything else you can add?" Bostwick stepped between us and attempted to answer for me, but the reporter, who obviously cared nothing for the mayor, interrupted him. "I think the viewers would like to hear from local law enforcement too, sir. Chief?"

Okay, how do I do this diplomatically? "I think what the mayor did, bringing in those early warning sirens, was the right move, but it really wasn't enough time. We will have to look at how we can improve that. I'm no scientist, but there has to be a way. As you know, Dauphin Island is only one square mile, and the bridge across Heron Pass is three miles long. It takes at least five minutes to get to the mainland with no traffic, and it's at least twice that during an evacuation. Sometimes the bridge can get pretty backed up."

"Are you going to evacuate the island, Chief?"

"No, not at this time. I'm thinking we'll have the report from the geologists and will then know what the next steps are. No problem with local oil rigs, no major construction. I can't understand what else it could be. But as I said, I am no scientist."

"What are you focusing on now, Chief Castille?"

"Right now, all our efforts are focused on finding the two missing islanders. Beyond that, I don't know. I guess wait and see what the USGS tells us and be ready." Kendra stood off camera waving at me. I took the opportunity to excuse myself. Mayor Bostwick glared at me, but what could he do but fire me later?

"Missing islanders? Can you give us the names and descriptions of the individuals? I'm sure we could help get the word out, Chief."

"I'll get them for you. I didn't know we were having a press conference, or I would have had that prepared. Give my staff a few minutes to gather the info. Will you please excuse me?"

Kendra covered her mouth and whispered to me, "One of the missing people, Emily LaFonte, has been found. She's alive, but just barely. Your friends Nike and Ramara dragged her out of the sea. She's on her way to the hospital on the mainland, but they want to talk to you. They saw something."

I glanced over my shoulder. Now there were two local stations and a national television station setting up for interviews. "Come on, let's talk in here."

Kendra waved Nik and Ramara over, and the four of us hustled past the growing crowd of media and into one of the unused rooms of the Dauphin Island Air Force Station. The place had been shuttered since the '80s, but recently the Coast Guard and local marine biologists had begun using it again. The buildings had been opened today and used for storage and meeting places. The room smelled like wet sand and old paint, but it was the best we could do for privacy at the moment.

Ramara whispered in Nik's ear, and she nodded at him. I didn't like seeing that one damn bit. "You need to tell me something?" I said, anxious to hurry this along. I had better things to do than watch the woman I was crushing on hook up with some other guy. And he wasn't even a guy. Aw, crap. Neither was I, not one hundred percent. She wasn't human either, for that matter. Kendra stared at me as if to say, *Get it together, Castille.*

"We thought you might like to know that Minerva is lurking in the waters off the island. She's here because of Meri."

I scratched my head and replaced my hat. I didn't have time to figure out puzzles. "What does that mean? What's Minerva? Some kind of fish? Bottom-line it, please. I kinda have my hands full, what with a tidal wave and all."

"Hey! She's trying to tell you that this isn't over. Minerva isn't a fish—she's a mermaid, and a very powerful one at that. She's not even supposed to be here. Meri is one of her shimmer."

"Shimmer?" Another stupid question. I was on a roll today.

"Yes, Cruise. That's what they call a group of mermaids—a shimmer. You're missing the point, though. Minerva caused the tidal wave—it was a warning shot, and there's more to come if we don't appease her."

Kendra broke into the conversation. "How do we do that?"

"She wants Meri. She obviously doesn't know what happened to her daughter." Nike chewed the inside of her lip and brushed a mass of brown tendrils out of her face. God, she was sexy. She had sand in her hair and had never looked more beautiful. *What the heck is wrong with me? This is no time to be thinking like a teenager.*

"The mermaid never came back, did she? What does Heliope say about this? Wasn't she a part of that?"

"She says she left Meri with the Order, but obviously that message didn't get to Minerva because she's here churning up the water and pretty pissed off. And I was Meri's friend. Minerva is going to hold me accountable for what happened to her." Nike paced the small room, kicking at a forgotten piece of paper.

"You sure know how to treat your friends," Kendra said under her breath, her short temper shining through. Even I wouldn't have said that, and there was nothing wrong with Nike's hearing. Ramara broke in to stop the inevitable argument.

"Hey, no finger-pointing right now, please. Listen, we didn't have to tell you a damn thing, but we're here. We want to help you protect what we have here—and the people, of course. Of all races. We'll find Heliope and see what else she can tell us about Meri. Just be prepared. If I were you, I would make sure everyone got off this island until we can figure out how to get rid of Minerva."

"How can we do that?" Kendra asked. "The mayor is never going to go for that."

"We just won't ask him. I don't need his permission to order an evacuation of the island."

Everyone looked uncertain, but I was adamant. "Seriously. I know what I'm talking about. Who here besides me went to the police academy?"

Kendra raised her hand with a glare.

"The point is, I can do this. I might be out of a job afterwards, but I can do it at least once. If it means keeping everyone safe, it's a no-brainer."

Nobody tried talking me out of it so I said, "I'll go out there now and give the order. Then when the place is empty, we can do what we have to do."

"Come on, Cruise. What? We're going to fight a mermaid? They are in the water. We're shifters, in case you didn't remember that. You haven't even experienced a full shift yet. And for your further information, we don't shift into sharks—we're wolves," Kendra said with a snort. She wasn't having any of this nonsense, as she liked to say. But it wasn't because she was fearful. Kendra had buckets full of brave. She was worried about how I'd handle my shifter powers in a fight...and she had every reason to be. I didn't have a clue. She continued, "There are going to be choppers everywhere, news media, even after you evacuate the island. You can't keep the press out, dude. And I'm sure none of this has escaped the Order, by the way," Kendra added authoritatively.

"Nobody says you have to be here," Nik snapped at her, totally misinterpreting Kendra's commentary. I heard Kendra growl, but I was pretty sure I was the only one who could discern it. Then I saw Nik's face.

Nope, I was wrong.

A scuffle outside the window broke up the potential catfight. I heard someone swear as they fell to the ground. I ran to the open window and stuck my head out. The jerky reporter was running around the corner. I only caught a glimpse of him, but his scent lingered behind. Kendra came up beside me sniffing too.

"Who was that? Or better yet, what was that?"

"The reporter, the one I was talking to earlier. The guy with the blond curly hair and expensive shoes. Chris Hanson."

She whispered to me, "Don't trust him. He's not our kind."

"But he helped me earlier. If it weren't for him, nobody would have known we have people missing."

Kendra nodded. "Fine, but be careful. He's a different kind of shifter."

"I better make the announcement before the media does it for me. Let's catch up later. Call me, Nik."

"Sure. Thanks, Cruise." No hug goodbye. No kiss for luck.

I walked out, leaving Nik and Ramara behind, but Kendra was right beside me every step of the way. If nothing else, at least there was that.

Chapter Nine—Nike

Second Wave

S "I don't like her."

"I think that's pretty apparent, but we've got bigger fish to try."

Crazy to think that in the midst of all the "crazy" I could smile, but Ramara made it easy. "I think you mean fry."

He chuckled. "I see. Well, that too." He was hanging out the open window now and not listening to me at all. "The wolves were right—that was a strange scent. And here's another question, how did our spy get up here without a ladder? This building is a good three feet off the ground. And why would he go to all that trouble?"

So strange hearing Cruise referred to as a wolf. I didn't know what to think about all that. I'd not met any shifters until recently. I'd heard of them, of course, but I imagined them to be hairy and kind of crazy. Cruise was neither of those things. I looked down and saw that Ramara was right about the height. "That is weird. Maybe he had a friend helping him. A tall friend with big shoulders." I nudged his arm playfully and said, "We better go find Heliope. We don't have time to get involved with their shifter-drama."

"Right." We left the building, skirted the crowd and made a beeline for my car.

"Oh my goodness. I left poor Springer in the house today. Poor guy. I hope Heliope thought to let him out. If not, he's probably torn my house up, hopefully not as bad as the last time." I started to say more but remembered sweeping and finding the scroll in the garbage can.

All the power was out on the island, and I allowed myself a second to glance at my store. It felt like I hadn't been there in so long.

Ramara cast an eye in that direction too. "Looks okay from here."

"Good." I jetted onto Chaumont, slid into the gravel driveway and hopped out. I heard Springer barking excitedly at my arrival. "Come on in." I dug for my keys, which were still in my jeans. Good thing I took them off before I hopped in the ocean. Oh right, he saw me in my underwear. Oh well, he'd already seen me in less than that.

"Coming, Springer!" I jiggled the key in the lock and opened the door, then Springer blew past me without so much as a courtesy bark. "Wow, you must really have to go." But he didn't make for the garden. He shot down the beach toward the marina. "Springer! Come back here!"

"You want me to go after him?"

I didn't know what to do. Where was Heliope? "He'll probably be right back, just smells something interesting. Heliope? You in here?" The house felt warm, even though it was the beginning of October. "Heliope?"

"Wasn't she coming back here?"

"I thought she was. But there's no sign of her. Where could she have gone?"

"Maybe to the shop?"

I hated leaving home so soon, but that was the only logical thing I could think of. Just then, someone knocked on my door. "Hold on a second," I said to Ramara, who was rummaging through my refrigerator.

I opened the door and found Jolly standing there. In a disappointed voice, he said, "Oh, hey."

"Hi, Jolly," I replied, feeling anxious. I didn't recall ever having him at my house before. "Something I can help you with?"

"There's been an evacuation, and I was making sure you knew about it."

"Yes, we just heard that. You closing up at the school?"

"Uh huh. Is Heliope around? I could use her help with something."

"Oh, shoot. No she's not, but I'll be sure and tell her you're looking for her, okay?"

He noticed Ramara, who had apparently found a sandwich in the fridge and was enjoying it while lingering behind me. I rolled my eyes and turned back to Jeff. "Anything else, Jolly?"

"No, I guess that's it. I think. No, there's something else." I saw him tense up, his eyes squeezed shut. He started breathing fast as if he might have a heart attack right on my front porch.

"Oh goodness! You okay? Sit in the rocker here."

"No, I have to tell you—the gate—Heliope's at the gate—she needs you to come now..." Then with a loud scream he collapsed in the rocker, panting harder than before.

"How do you know about the gate?" Ramara tossed the sandwich in the yard like I lived in a rundown old trailer park. I didn't think right now was the time to correct his behavior, but I would certainly mention it later.

"I'm not supposed to-tell-you..." He struggled to say each word, and then Ramara understood.

"It's the Order. He's the new gate guardian. We have to go now!"

"I'll grab the keys! Jolly, stay here. We'll be back soon! I hope!"

"No time for keys. I'll drive," Ramara said, scooping me up and taking off across the island at a dizzying speed. *What? I thought he couldn't do this anymore!*

I closed my eyes and enjoyed the closeness of him. It lasted only a few seconds because we were at the gate so fast my head was spinning. I doubted my dizziness was from his speed. *Good lord, you're being ridiculous,* I scolded myself. I tucked a hair behind my ear and stood at the gate, pretending to appraise it. No letters glowed over the top, and I didn't see Heliope anywhere. Ramara sat on a rock nearby and watched me.

"All the years, decades, centuries I've guarded the gate, and I've never been through it. I guess there's no time like the present." I looked up and down the beach and called her name. Nothing, not a sound. There weren't any seagulls either and no sign of Springer. "It looks all clear." He acted as if he didn't hear me. "Hey! Can you activate this thing or what?"

"You really mean you can't, princess?"

"You know I can't."

"Just say 'open sesame' and believe that it will open."

"What is wrong with you?" I didn't appreciate the sarcasm. He was just too dang moody lately. I looked up and down the rock formation, trying to find a clue as to how to open it. "Can you open this or not? Heliope needs us! You heard Jolly."

"Yes, I can open it. But maybe I don't want to."

I stomped in the sand toward him. "What do you mean you don't want to?" Before I could let him have it, something like a sonic boom sounded across the water. "What was that?" The island shook slightly under my feet. "Minerva?" I asked fearfully as I stared out across the water and saw nothing. No vicious mermaid queen rose out of the water to find me and drag me to the depths. It really could have been anything, including a sonic boom from one of the nearby military bases. After a few seconds of waiting for impending death, I saw nothing. Ramara stepped toward the water's edge to investigate, his blue tattoos gleaming slightly, but apparently he detected nothing either.

"I can't get in the gate without your help, Ramara. I can't sit back and let her..."

"Die? She's not going to die, Nik. And who's to say that Jolly sending you here isn't a trick? You can't trust anyone. Haven't you figured that out? You're too naïve for your own good."

"I *don't* trust them. But if she's not at home and not here, then where is she?" The water splashed under our feet now. *That's odd. It's not time for the tide to come in, is it?*

"How do I know? She's Heliope! Knowing her, she followed a butterfly through the Audubon Bird Trail. I'm sure she's safe."

"Sure? How can you be sure?" My face whitened despite the late afternoon sun. "You know something, don't you?" I stepped closer and asked him again. "Don't you?"

"What could I possibly know? I've been with you, remember?"

Another boom sounded in the Gulf, and this time the results were immediate. Out deep in the water a wave was building. I could see it. Waves like that appeared small from a distance—they actually were somewhat small until they approached shore and the water gathered up in a heap. There was now no water under our feet at all. "We don't have time to play games. I thought you were here to help me!"

He gripped me by the arms and stared down at me with an intensity I'd never seen from him before. "You don't get it, Nik. If I open that gate, I may not be able to come back to you. I'd be gone forever. Is that what you want?"

I stared up at him, his wheat-colored hair tossing across his light-colored eyes, eyes that peered deeply into mine. Any other time I'd want to get lost in them. Then I got it. It was the Order and the scroll and his status. This was about us.

Instinctively I put my arms around him and hugged with all my might, just as he'd done for me when I needed comforting. But this was more than comfort from a friend. I meant this. He seemed surprised at my gesture but didn't stop me. I breathed him in, wishing this moment would last for eternity. But it could not. Another boom shook the island, and I heard my dog somewhere in the distance barking his head off. "Springer!" I said as I tried to pull away. "He could be in danger!" "No, don't look, Nik."

"Look at what?" As I spoke, I felt the wind blowing off the ocean and heard the water draw back behind me. "I have to see." I didn't really need to, did I? Death by tidal wave. It may or may not have killed us; that much was uncertain at this point. But he was right, I didn't have to watch the water come crashing down on us, crushing our bones. He refused to release me, and I buried my face in his chest with a sob. I whispered his name. I was unsure what we were facing, but at least we would face it together.

"No! I cannot allow this. You cannot die!" I heard him shout. He uttered the words, the secret words that opened the gate. Suddenly we were falling, the beach and Springer and the deadly wave behind us.

We lay on the ground together in the fog. For the first time ever in my long life, I would see the Order.

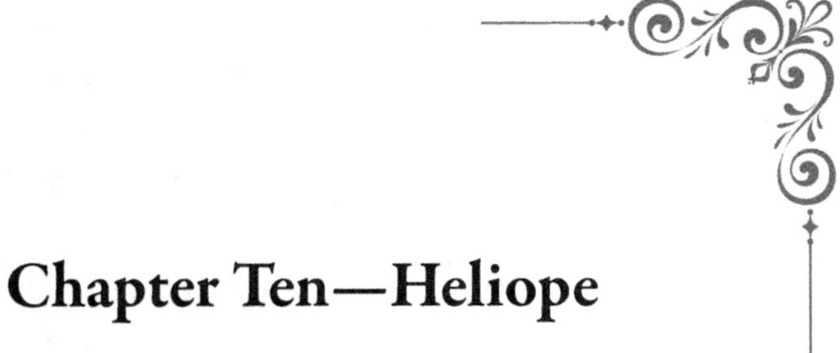

Chapter Ten—Heliope

Old Woman Faydra, I know you are here. Do not hide from me.

I batted at the fog, as if I could shoo it away. That was impossible; it stuck to my hair and skin like a cold, clingy garment. It made my skin crawl, and I had the feeling that if I allowed it to, the fog would hide me forever. Never before had it been so thick, not here where the sun used to shine on the courtyard and temple continuously. The first time I came to see the Order, after Agrios took me as his wife, the Secret Temple shone like a bright ball of light, bathed as it was in golden sunshine. Each visit after that was much different. The fog began to encroach on that sunny place, creeping in from the woods that surrounded it, then into the plazas and hidden villas that were the homes of the Higher Orders.

Then over the long years, members of the Higher Order began to disappear in the fog. One by one they vanished until only six remained. Six to lead Oceanid kind, and no end in sight to the fog. The Order pulled from the races to fill those leadership roles, but the fog had done something else too.

It affected those of the original Order—those that still remained. And it affected them deeply. Faydra became crueler, darker, more desperate to control everything under her influence. Even her eyes darkened in color. It was almost as if that beautiful being of light no longer existed. Somehow the unholy fog had replaced it, and now darkness ruled.

To make matters even more troubling, Faydra no longer appeared to me as herself but used the bodies of humans to communicate her will on earth. That was very different from the way things used to be. The old Faydra, the strong, powerful Faydra, would never dream of relying on a human for help of any sort.

And now, according to Ramara, Faydra killed her human hosts—whether intentionally or not, that was an evil act. Not that it mattered, but I did not approve. Not at all.

The fog thickened so much that I could barely see the stairs now. Those stairs would lead me to the highest platform in the temple, a place where we used to watch the constellations move and interact with one another.

How overwhelmed I had been with it all when Agrios brought me here! He'd laughed at that and told me a secret. This was nothing compared to the Order's former glory. The truth became apparent to me eventually. The Higher Order now dwelled on a veiled island, having been evicted from the high and lofty Mount Olympus and other such exquisite places around the globe. But for all my questions, I would learn no more about it. Agrios would not say who evicted the pantheon of gods and goddesses from their so-called eternal homes. But the world had changed. Men had changed and didn't need the small gods and the jealous goddesses. They no longer revered Zeus, who changed into golden sand to slip through a lock to lie with the fairest of the land. No longer needed to hear the will of the god from Hermes, the Invisible Messenger. Men became jealous over their wives and thoughts, and their hearts turned to a different God. One who became God of everything, to those who believed in Him.

Faydra, answer me. I need the mermaid, the one I gave to you. Minerva has come, and she wants her daughter. Mercy, mercy, Faydra! Many lives are at stake—many supernaturates will be destroyed if we do not appease her. I must return the mermaid to her home!

For a long time I stood in the center of the temple waiting to hear her deep, sultry voice. All of a sudden, a light flared behind me. Someone quietly lit the Bowls of Attendance, indicating that the Order was now convened. I breathed a sigh of relief. Someone had heard me after all. "Who is there?" I said with my mouth as a human would.

"I am here, Willful One. I think you were married to Agrios for too long, for you have many of his characteristics. You think about things that you should not, Heliope, Daughter of Dionysus."

Her label mocked me, for I was not related by blood to Dionysus. He was Agrios' father, not mine. "What I think about is Thessalonike and how she will die if I do not help her. Please give me the mermaid, Faydra. I will pay the price."

"Oh? The price may be too high for you, Heliope." I could not discern her in the fog, but I felt her move around me, heard her garments rustling in the temple as she lit the many bowls. It created a dull glow in the hallowed halls of the council room. "You want me to help Thessalonike when she's thinking of betraying the Order?"

"What? What are you talking about?" I demanded.

"Don't play the fool with me. I am referring to Thessalonike and the eloi—they are not permitted."

"Not permitted to what? Kiss? Make love? Marry? If you think you can stop love, Faydra, you don't know anything about the world we live in."

She stalked through the fog, and it parted obediently as she came toward me. "No, it is *you* who do not understand, Heliope. Self-centered, selfish Heliope who finally developed a conscience and a maternal instinct! How un-goddesslike of you, my dear." Her sharp voice surprised me. I said nothing, hoping I would not irritate her further. I needed Meri. The fog pooled around us again. "You see this? You see how we can barely see one another? How do you think it got here?"

"I haven't got a clue, Faydra." I could see her as she stepped within inches of me. No human host needed today, Faydra was herself with her famous red curly hair, long and flowing down her back, tanned skin, very wide green eyes and bow lips that shined without the need of any human cosmetics. She wore a half shirt and a long skirt, red with gold ribbons at the hems and sleeves, in the fashion of the goddesses of old.

"Corruption. The corruption of the Order caused this. Now there are three of us, Heliope. Three to carry on and lead the races, and yet you come here with your petty demands and all your pride. Yes, that had always been your problem. Pride. That is your corruption."

If she'd seen me earlier, being pummeled by mermaid tails at the bottom of the ocean, she wouldn't have thought I was too prideful at all. Before I could defend myself, she spoke again.

"I will not let the Order disappear forever. We will deal with this corruption wherever we find it. Are you willing, Heliope, to root out the corruption within you?"

She had not moved, but I felt pressure around my throat as if an invisible hand were squeezing it. I could do nothing to stop it. Without knowing what she had in mind, I answered fearfully, "Yes, Faydra."

Now she was so close I could see the gold dust shimmering in her hair. "Good, Heliope. With your purification, we are one step closer to making the Order a place of light once again." She released her grip on me and purred in my ear, "I am going to send you back to Thessalonike, and you can help her to your heart's content now. However, when I call on you, you must answer." Faydra doused the lighting stick by blowing on it expertly.

"Really? What about the mermaid?"

"She's already there. She's been there." Faydra was shocked by my stupidity. "Haven't you seen her?"

"No, I haven't."

"Hmm...that makes me wonder about your magic, Heliope. If you can't discern a mermaid from another creature..."

"She's enchanted!"

"There is hope for you yet. Now go home."

Faydra backed away, blowing out the Bowls of Attendance as she departed the temple. I walked down the long hall and the stairs, thinking about what I had learned. I carefully guarded my thoughts to avoid being overheard by her or one of the others who lingered in the mist.

I hoped I could find the gate quickly and go home, but before I even made it to the walkway I heard the gate scrape open and saw the purple letters glowing above it. Who was this?

As I ran toward it, my bones began to ache like never before. Almost there now! A few more steps! I encouraged myself to continue on despite the aches and pains in my legs and arms. What was this pain? Some kind of effect of the fog?

The gate glowed brighter as the door opened. On the ground in front of me fell two people—Ramara and Thessalonike.

Chapter Eleven—Cruise

Red Slicker

Without saying a word, Kendra jumped out of the car and bolted. The evacuation was moving slowly now because some fool's car had broken down. Rather than trying to roll the vehicle onto the shoulder, the car's owner had abandoned it and was now running down the bridge, uncaring that he was leaving the rest of the island's residents locked in danger. I saw the wave breaking out across the water, and I wasn't the only one. People were screaming, kids were pointing and crying. The wave wasn't a threat to just the island but to the bridge as well. I wasn't sure how tall the wave would be, but it sure as heck looked imposing and dangerous.

"Kendra!" I shouted as she put the car in neutral and began pushing on it. I got behind the bumper and was quickly joined by two others who helped us ease the abandoned car off the road.

"Push, damn it!" she yelled at us, sounding desperate and angry.

In a few seconds we moved it, and then she shouted, "Run! Get going now!" The wave was about to hit us, and there wasn't a chance any of us would cross the bridge in time. The only thing we could do was get people to the top of the bridge and pray the wave passed under us. I bolted for the squad car, grabbed the speaker and yelled, "Get to the top of the bridge! Please, everyone move quickly and help your neighbor! Go now!"

I started pulling people out of cars and shoving them toward the top of the bridge. "It's coming! Get moving!" I yelled at Mrs. Marsh, the mayor's secretary, who insisted on dragging her heavy-as-heck purse with her. I moved to the next car, Kendra beside me in her shiny red raincoat. She reminded me of Little Red Riding Hood. I couldn't help but laugh at the irony.

"Go! Run to the top!" Kendra shouted to an older couple who were doing their best to obey her. The tall wave moved closer, the water an eerie green with a nasty thick foam on top.

"Kendra! Run!" I grabbed her hand, and together we made for the highest point on the bridge along with the others who were waiting for the wave to crest. Then with a supernatural thud, the wave struck the bridge and washed over the empty cars below us. The force of the water knocked Kendra to the ground, but I didn't let her go. I pulled her close and covered her with my body, trying to shield her from the painful blow. The water hit me so hard it nearly took the wind out of me, but beyond that I was okay. After it rolled over us and the water poured off the side of the concrete bridge, I lay on top of her, panting for breath as salty water streamed off me onto her face. She didn't move under me, and I feared the worst.

"You okay?"

"I think so. Are we alive?" she groaned.

I grinned at her. "Well, yeah. Don't you feel alive?"

"No, I feel like I've been drowned—and crushed."

"I was trying to protect you, ungrateful woman," I joked with her. I clumsily climbed off of her and helped her to her feet.

After we caught our breath, she mumbled, "Thanks." When we were sure that everyone would be okay, Kendra and I stood on the side of the bridge and watched Minerva's wave crush the west end of the island.

"Oh God," I said as I watched the Pirateer wash away. The half of a pirate ship quickly sank into the tumultuous waters of the Gulf of Mexico. I hated to see the place go; it had once been my home away from home. "She's going to tear up the entire island if we don't give her the mermaid."

"Or Thessalonike," Kendra said. She didn't look at me, just watched the water ruthlessly pound the shoreline.

"What? No way are we giving her Thessalonike. That's out of the question."

"Regardless, the mermaid queen isn't going away anytime soon. I'm afraid we've just begun to see the wrath of Minerva."

"Nothing to do but get to the gate and find Nik. Maybe she's found Heliope."

"What about the mayor? Won't he be waiting for you on the other side? I'd hate to see your career end before it got started." She followed me to the squad car. I began shouting to people to get back in their cars and head for land. We had to move them quickly in case there was another wave. Who knew what Minerva had in mind? The islanders didn't waste any time following instructions this time. Even the high-maintenance Mrs. Marsh put some pep in her step. "He's arranged another press conference, and I'm sure he's going to make you explain yourself. Bold move ordering an evac without consulting him first, Cruise. Maybe too bold."

"Yeah, he'll probably want my badge, but I'm not ready to give it up yet. I've still got a job to do, and I plan on doing it. Now that this wave has passed, let's head back before he takes the badge and the car—and my deputy."

Soaking wet, she climbed into the seat beside me and put on her seat belt. "Which one would you miss the most, Chief?"

I turned the key in the ignition and without looking at her turned the car south, back to Dauphin Island. "You. I'd miss you most, Kendra Tragic." She didn't say a word, but I could see her smile out of the corner of my eye. She flipped on the sirens, and we headed back to Cadillac Avenue.

Chapter Twelve—Nike

Older Than

"Why are you here? Go now! Back through the gate!" A bent figure scurried toward us as Ramara and I struggled to stand upright again. I had no stomach for traveling back through so soon, but this character demanded that I move. And that voice seemed all too familiar.

"Heliope? Is that you?" I squinted as a patch of fog cleared between us.

"No time for talking! We have to go back—the Order can't see you here together!"

"Heliope?" I asked again stupidly. The voice was my stepmother's, but the figure it belonged to didn't look like her, not in the least. This was an *old* woman, not the vibrant Heliope with illuminated hair and an eternally trim figure.

"Let's go, Nike," she scolded me, practically shoving Ramara and me back through the gate. As we stepped through again, I floated for a few seconds and then fell to the ground in an unceremonious heap; my innards quivered with the shift in time, space or whatever else the Order manipulated to make such travel possible. I sat on all fours in the wet sand of Dauphin Island, waiting for the world to stop moving while Ramara stood over me protectively.

Heliope collapsed on a rock nearby and tried to catch her breath. "I don't feel well," she complained. I had never heard her complain about ill health in the hundreds of years we'd known one another. Except for the occasional hangover.

"What did they do to you?" Ramara asked incredulously. I finally glanced up and couldn't hide my shock.

"Heliope?" I crawled to her and looked up in her face. Yes, those were her lovely, quick eyes, but her face was wrinkled and spotted, her skin crepey and saggy.

"What? Why are you looking at me like I have two heads? Oh my God! Do I have two heads?" Then she caught a glimpse of her hands and screamed. She rose to her wobbly feet and cried aloud, "Faydra! Faydra did this to me! Is my face bad? Is my face old and ugly like my hands?" She tried to run to the water's edge, perhaps to see her reflection, but it was churning and sloshing and not safe for anyone to venture into at the moment. Even an immortal. If she was still that.

"Heliope, we must go. Minerva has sent two waves already. Another is sure to follow until this situation is resolved. Did you learn anything about the mermaid?" Ramara's hands were on his hips, a move he often used when he wanted to gain control of a conversation. It wasn't working at the moment.

Still staring at her hands, she whimpered and did not answer. We heard another boom shake the island.

"Please, Heliope. I need your help. This is troubling, I know," I tried to soothe her, "but we have to find Meri, if she is alive after all. Lives depend on it."

"Faydra—yes, I saw Faydra, Ramara. The real Faydra. I saw her face to face. She says that Meri is here on the island." Fascinated and repulsed by her hands, she touched them and rubbed them constantly.

"Really? Where? Did she say where?" I felt hopeful but only for a second.

"No."

Exasperated, I struggled to find the words I needed. None came. My phone rang in my pocket and I saw Cruise's name pop up on the screen, but it was Kendra on the phone.

"Hi, Nike. We just finished the evacuation and are headed back your way. Any word on Heliope?"

"She's here, says Meri is on the island somewhere, but I haven't seen her. I'm about to head into the water. If she's here, that's where she'd be." I rolled my eyes as I listened to Kendra relay the information to Cruise. *Why didn't you just put me on speakerphone instead of playing this power trip?*

"Obviously we're not great swimmers, but we can take the police boat out to keep an eye on you. We'll meet you at the marina in fifteen minutes. That mermaid has to be found."

It was a half-assed plan, but it was the only one we had at the moment. I could tell by Ramara's scowl that he did not approve, but I didn't care. "Sounds good. See you there."

Ramara didn't offer an objection, which seemed weird. He always had something to say about these things. But maybe it was the only way. Heliope appeared to wither before us. She complained again about her bones hurting...I didn't want to tell her, but it appeared that she was getting older by the minute.

"I can't make that walk."

"If you'll allow me, I will carry you."

She made no objection, and Ramara scooped her up like she was a dried leaf. We didn't make the run at supernatural speed, as Heliope wasn't up to that. We walked quickly along the shore the half mile to the marina, amazed at all the water on land. It looked like there had been a hurricane.

"I didn't get a chance to thank you for what you did, so thank you."

"You are welcome, princess," he said matter-of-factly.

"I don't need to remind you again that I'm not a princess anymore, do I? My friends call me Nik."

"I can't help the way I think about you." My heart caught in my throat at his words.

"If you two don't shut up, I'm going to die. I may die anyway."

We were on the pier now, and I could see the police launch easing toward us in the water. "You aren't going to die, Heliope. If it were possible to kill you, believe me, somebody would have already done it."

"Is that supposed to be funny, girl?" she said weakly as Ramara set her down gently on the boat. I scrambled and found a blanket to put around her shoulders. She was complaining about being cold, even though it was a nice sunny day. Well, except for the tidal waves. Cruise and Kendra tied their boat next to ours and came aboard.

"Oh, hello, ma'am. Did you get stuck out here? Didn't you hear there was an evacuation? Is there someone we should call for you?" Cruise squatted down in front of her, talking loudly as if she were deaf.

"Cruise," I broke in. He waved his hand at me and patted her hand.

"It's going to be o-kay, ma'am."

"If I had the energy, I would punch you in the face, stupid boy." Heliope wrapped her blanket tighter around her shoulders and ignored him.

Open-mouthed, Cruise looked in my direction.

"Minerva do this?" Kendra asked fearfully. Yes, I could see why this kind of spell would frighten her. She relied too heavily on her looks. At least her ponytail was sagging and her cherry red lip gloss had washed away, I thought nastily. I felt pretty good about my uncharitable thoughts until I saw Ramara's face. *How many times do I have to ask him to stop reading my mind?*

"We need to get out on the water," I said, hoping to defuse the situation. "I can't understand why Meri hasn't shown herself to me. That's just not like her. Still, if she's here, I'll find her."

"She's enchanted," Heliope said in a scratchy voice. "That's what the old witch told me before she stole my youth. I don't know what it means, but Faydra said she's here."

"Here but enchanted? What could that mean? That Faydra's hidden Meri somewhere?"

"No time to speculate," Kendra said, tapping on her phone. "We've gotten an earthquake warning from the USGS. There's another wave out there past Mon Luis. Headed this way. If we're going to do this, we might as well do it now. I hope you know what you're talking about, siren."

"I hope so too."

"Better get going, then."

Next thing I knew, Springer was bouncing down the pier barking furiously. "Oh my gosh! Springer! Come here, boy! Where have you been? I'm so happy to see you." His hair was covered in sand as if he'd just crawled out of the ocean or almost drowned in it. He bounded on board and jumped in my lap. I sobbed as I held him. "Boy, I'm going to ground you for life if you don't quit running away. Are you thirsty?" His pink tongue hung out of his mouth, and I scurried below deck with him to find him some water as Ramara eased out of the marina. The two boats motored in tandem. I didn't need to go out far, just far enough to launch into the Down Deep. Minerva might be waiting for me, but it was a chance I had to take for my friends and for the people of Dauphin Island.

"You stay here. I've got to find a lost friend." He barked at me as if he wanted to volunteer his help, but I patted his head before kissing it quickly. "Yuck! You stink, Springer. If I live through this, you will be getting a serious bubble bath. Wish me luck. If for some reason I don't make it back, you take care of Heliope. She needs you."

He barked excitedly and padded alongside me as I tried to slip out the door. He wasn't having any of it. "No, boy. You stay here." I closed the door behind me, pushing on it hard to lock it into place. He barked continuously as I jogged up the stairs. The noise would get on Heliope's nerves, but there wasn't anything I could do about that.

"He okay?" Ramara asked.

"No obvious cuts. Just thirsty and mad to be left below. Take me out to the point, and I'll dive out there. Any sign of Minerva?"

"Not yet, but she's around. How's Heliope?" I glanced over my shoulder and could see her whispering. Probably working on reversing the enchantment.

"About as you would expect. Faydra did a number on her. I had no idea she still had such power."

He glanced out over the water and grabbed his binoculars. "Hell! There she is! Minerva has spotted us."

"I'll have to get out now, then. Maybe I can find Meri before she kills us all. Heliope! Snap out of it! She's here!"

"Meri?"

"No! Minerva! Get ready."

"Ready for what? What am I supposed to do, Thessalonike? Just look at me!" She let the blanket fall to the ground and stood shakily.

I pulled off my shoes and pulled my hair up in the scrunchie I had in my pocket. "You can start by cutting the crap! We don't have time for you to feel sorry for yourself. Make yourself useful and whip up some protection spells or something. You're the goddess here. Where's your creativity?"

She snapped her bony fingers, and I was happy to see her excited, if only for a second. "Okay, let me think." She plopped back down on the padded cushion, chewing on her fingernail.

"Great, you do that."

Ramara anchored the boat and walked toward me. "I'm going with you."

"Not this time."

"You don't command me, princess."

Heliope paced the deck of the boat, whispering enchantments for our protection, while Springer barked even louder. "If something goes wrong, I want you to get our friends out of here." I touched his arm as I pleaded with him.

"And if something goes wrong out there, it won't matter. I am going with you." He pulled off his shirt and shoes, and I tried to look away. Now wasn't the time to be drooling over Ramara. Besides, Cruise was just on the next boat. What the heck was wrong with me?

"Fine, have it your way. But if Heliope sinks your boat, don't say I didn't warn you."

I waved Cruise over and pointed into the distance. "Get your life vests on! We're going in to find Meri!"

Kendra gave us a thumbs-up and scrambled to get the vests. Cruise gave Ramara a disapproving look but didn't say anything. Probably a good thing at this point.

"Get ready!" Heliope screamed at us.

"For what?" I yelled back. Minerva was still a half mile away. What was I missing?

"For this!" she shouted with a big grin. Next thing I knew, showers of purple sparks were falling around both boats, hiding us from Minerva, her dangerous green waters and her bloodthirsty shimmer of mermaids.

Not a bad way to start a fight.

Chapter Thirteen—Nike

The Boss

Ramara's athletic body slid through the water beside me. He briefly took my hand and squeezed it. I squeezed back. I dove deep into the water as his tattoos glowed and as his wings began to emerge. He hovered above me as I called to Meri.

Meri? Can you hear me? Meri! It is Thessalonike!

I heard nothing. No small animals scrabbling across the ocean floor searching for scraps. No wide-winged stingrays floating like lazy sea angels. No sharks, no fish. Nothing but empty waters churned asunder by the angry mermaid queen. I called again.

Meri! I need you, my friend! Friend needs you now! Where are you?

I plowed through the old shipwreck, the one the sea lab had sunk here as an artificial reef. It was one of Meri's favorite places to play. Perched near the top of a deep crevasse, the ship was anchored in place, but as I paddled closer, I noticed that it had moved a few feet, probably due to Minerva's recent onslaught of waves. Plunging through the open portal, I hoped to find Meri hiding somewhere in the ship, hopefully uninjured and with all her faculties. How could I not know she was here? The water felt warm on my skin until I reached the inner parts of the ship. Such an empty place now.

Everything in the ocean had better sense than me. Better sense than to be in the water right now with Minerva pushing ever closer to the island.

Meri, please! Where are you?

I scouted the remaining rooms and found nothing. Not a blond hair or a lost treasure—no sign of Meri. A shadow passed by the window. Thinking it was Ramara, I swam toward it until I felt something tug at my leg. Spinning about now, I could see Ramara behind me, his wings half-closed, pointing toward the window.

The shadow was a mermaid! Who knew how long Heliope's spell would remain in place? If it wasn't already busted apart like tissue paper under Minerva's power.

A boom echoed through the ship. It wasn't soul-shaking like the previous booms, but it shook my body through and through. Ramara stared at me as if he were trying to communicate with me, but I couldn't hear a thing. Only the sound of scraping metal—the mermaids were trying to shove us over the edge!

I swam to the portal to see how many there were. Seven or eight beautiful, fierce-looking mermaids swam in front of the windows, thrashing their tails against the metal hull of the boat. They had strange-looking weapons but not the strength to move this boat. Then I saw the green explosion of light hit the side of the ship.

It was Minerva! She focused her water power and slammed into the side of the boat. No doubt now that she knew we were here. No doubt she was playing for keeps.

Meri! Friend needs you now!

Desperation rose up within me. My friends above the water would die! Ramara would be hurt or killed! I could not save any of them! Sorrow and grief washed over me, and I began to sink to the floor of the ship.

Ramara tugged my hand. He had my attention now. Cradling my head in his hands, he stared at me with his piercing eyes. I could hear his thoughts as clearly as I could feel the despair.

No! That is part of her magic. No despair. Let's make a break for it! Let me carry you!

I nodded weakly and called one last time: *Please, Meri!*

Hold me tight, Thessalonike. We will live together or die together, but at least we will be together.

I put my arms around his neck, the effects of Minerva's magic weakening my resolve by the second. I *should* die—I deserved it. I should slip off into the nothingness and end it all. I should drown myself!

With a burst of rebellious anger, Ramara dove through the open top hatch, uncaring that four mermaids had spotted him and were driving toward us at breakneck speed. I pointed over his shoulder, but he did not look back.

Don't look, Thessalonike!

Up we went—up so fast through the briny water that it felt for a few horrible seconds as if we were sinking. I clung to Ramara as we approached the surface of the water. Fifty feet, twenty feet—ten feet! Two mermaids with gleaming green tails charged toward us from below, their faces the picture of hatred and revenge, claws extended, spears gleaming. As the distance between the sunken ship and us grew, the stronger I became. I clamped my hands over Ramara's ears and screamed a few high notes of a dirge. It had the desired effect. I watched with satisfaction the mermaids' painful response; the blood seeped out of their ears, and their faces contorted in pain. Then with an angry smile I watched them spiral back down. They weren't dead, not by a long shot, but I had successfully reminded them that I was a siren and not some wimpy human girl.

With his hand wrapped around my waist, Ramara hoisted me above the water. I broke the water with unexpected force. We landed on the boat but didn't hesitate. I ran to the other side of the ship to see Cruise and Kendra struggling. The smaller police launch was now the focus of Minerva's attention. "Heliope! Help them!"

"There is nothing I can do! I can't protect both boats!" she said in honest exasperation. She was drenched through and through and looked more frail then she had when we made our dive.

"Then we'll have to bring them here!"

Ramara shouted, "No! They need to go back! The shifters are no match for a shimmer of angry mermaids—Heliope's magic can't protect them! They are out of their league here, Nik." As if he agreed, Springer howled below us. Ramara hadn't steered me wrong before, and now wasn't the time to argue with him.

"Fine, let's get them to shore!"

Kendra clung to Cruise as another wave rocked their boat. And for the first time, I didn't feel ill, or jealous or bitchy. This was right! No matter what happened, Cruise would always be my friend, and he deserved to live and be happy. Even if that wasn't with me. I glanced over my shoulder and gave Ramara an apologetic look as I plunged back in the water.

"No! Nik!" I heard him yell over the roar of the waves. There was a good twenty feet between us, not enough to be safe. It was totally possible that Minerva was trying to smash our boats together. Somewhere in the distance I heard a helicopter hovering, but with the constant barrage of ocean spray, I couldn't tell where it was.

"Look! It's Nik! Help me, Kendra!" Cruise tossed the ring toward me, but I didn't grab it. I bobbed above the water and yelled at him.

"Go back to shore, Cruise! You can't be here! I'll protect you, but you won't have long. Go!"

He leaned against the edge of the boat and yelled back at me, but I couldn't discern the words. Kendra tugged at him with tears in her eyes, and for the first time since I'd met her, I could see that she was truly fearful. She was a smart girl—she should be afraid. Minerva's green glow began to surround me, and I turned my attention to her, the mermaids swirling closer to me now. I dove down, hoping Cruise would actually listen for a change. I sang a few more notes, repelling the weaker mermaids easily. The older, stronger ones didn't move back for long.

Please, Ramara! Stay out of the water, just for a few minutes!

I sang again and heard the police launch crank and putter away. As Minerva approached, I could hear her anger, feel it surround me in the green water. I sang a few more notes, but it wasn't effective. Not at all. The luminous green water spread around me like a fog. Then I heard the splash. Ramara dove beside me, his face a mask of determination. He held my hand again, and I looked at him hopelessly. Now that he was here, I couldn't sing. I could hurt him, or worse yet kill him. I'd already proved that my siren song had a horrible effect on him. Except when I was drunk.

Suddenly Ramara wasn't Ramara anymore. He transformed into a mermaid with a glowing blue tail—and so did I. I gasped, and he grinned at me and gave me a thumbs-up.

Heliope glamor.

I grinned back and sent him a determined thought. *Let's do this!* Hopefully Cruise and Kendra were safely out of the way.

We swam into the shimmer, and they accepted our presence without question, focused as they were on destroying me. Minerva hovered near us, and I shivered despite my newfound determination.

Find her, kill her. Revenge, kill, wound, scar!

How was it possible that I could hear her? Had Heliope's transformation worked that well? That was definitely a change for the better. Ramara and I nodded at each other and charged toward two of the weaker mermaids, using our tails to thrash them in the abdomen. I swirled around the stunned mermaid and hit her again. She tumbled head over tail a few feet and then was joined by her sister. Ramara and I plunged down below the green water and reemerged together, targeting two new mermaids. These were stronger, but they had not witnessed our earlier attack and had no idea what hit them. I got cocky with this attack and ended the tail slap with a punch in the face.

Evidently the mermaids were crying out to Minerva, for she changed direction and came toward us.

Intruder! Enemy! Daughters! Minerva screeched in anger and raised her hand as if she were about to blast us with her green-tinted energy. However, the mermaid queen hesitated, unsure who had hurt her daughters.

Feeling some rage of my own, I launched myself against the nearest mermaid, slapping her and punching her. *No more hiding! No more running! You want me? Here I am!*

I grabbed a second stunned mermaid and pressed my lips against her ear. I blasted a note and watched her rock with pain. Minerva saw me now. The glamor magic faded, and Ramara and I reverted to our true forms.

As quick as lightning, Minerva launched her power at us, the green water shooting in a stream and striking me in the chest with as much force as any tidal wave could have. I tumbled, my chest burned and my heart pumped faster. Ramara raced after me, putting himself between me and the queen of the mermaids. A boom shook the water, the soul-shaking boom. The shimmer gathered around her as they approached, grinning and gathering tighter and tighter. I didn't have any idea what they had planned, but whatever it was wouldn't be good. Not by any stretch of the imagination.

Ramara took my hand, but I caught my second wind. I was ready to end this! He shook his head and grabbed me, flying us to the boat. He too was injured, and for the first time I could see that he was bleeding from the ear. Obviously he hadn't escaped my siren's song. The boat shook, and the water around us turned green. The skies had darkened; whether by some magic or just bad weather, I could not tell. I tried to catch my breath, and Heliope hugged me as tightly as she could.

I hugged her back and said, "Thank you for what you did."

She patted my shoulder. "It's not over, I'm afraid. Here she comes, above the water now. I'm sorry, Thessalonike. I tried."

"I know you did, Heliope."

"Grab a flare gun!" Ramara shouted at me, but I didn't budge. It was me she wanted. I'd have to surrender. I had to make a deal. Springer barked again, and I felt my heart break.

"Take care of my dog, Heliope." I clutched her hand, ready to launch myself off the boat again, when Springer burst out of the cabin and ran on deck. As he ran toward me, his image blurred as if he were a hologram.

Then Springer wasn't Springer anymore. He was Meri!

Wait a minute. Springer is Meri?

Meri threw herself overboard and into the crashing water. Suddenly the waves became still and the green cloud of water became less bright. Minerva lingered, but she'd spotted her daughter—her now-human daughter. Meri didn't stay down long; she bobbed back up gasping for air. The green water completely dissipated now, and the shimmer of mermaids disappeared into the depths. There was no one left but Meri. She had no tail, no Oceanid powers. She was drowning.

"Oh no! Meri!" I dove in and swam beneath my friend. Sliding my arms under hers, I dragged her back to the surface. She gasped and choked, but her face was the picture of abject sadness. Not relief. Not joy at seeing me. I knew why. Minerva had nearly wiped out the island to find her, but after she saw that Meri was now human, by some weird magic, she completely rejected her. No words had to be spoken between us to know what had just happened.

As we climbed back up the ladder and onto the boat, one mermaid returned. She was a petite blonde, like Meri. I'd wounded her earlier, but she didn't care about my presence. She came to see her sister. To say goodbye.

Her head bobbed above the water for a minute; the two stared at one another sadly, and if any words were spoken, I didn't hear them. The mermaid raised a pale hand above the water and waved once to Meri. She returned the gesture and watched her sister disappear below the surface of the now-still water. For a long time, the four of us sat on the boat trying to catch our breath and get our bearings. Heliope was exhausted; her glamor magic had finally faded. Ramara had more than a few bruises. Meri seemed lost.

To think, Meri had been with me all this time, and I had never known it. How stupid I was! We'd probably never know how it all happened unless Faydra told us, for Meri still couldn't speak. And now she could not share her emotions as she used to. We hugged, and I held her for a long time as we finally turned the boat back to the island. I could see the police launch safely back at the marina, thankfully. Cruise and Kendra anxiously waited for us.

Kendra gave us a ride home in the police car, and Meri sat in the back seat and stared at the ocean. I wondered if she regretted her choice or if she'd ever even had one.

Did any of us where the Order was concerned? Although we'd won the day, they hadn't helped us. Despite my five hundred years of faithful service to this island and the gate. And Meri had been by my side the entire time. What had she gained from all that devotion?

I couldn't help but feel that soon a day of reckoning would be upon us. Choices would have to be made. Hard choices.

What else would we lose?

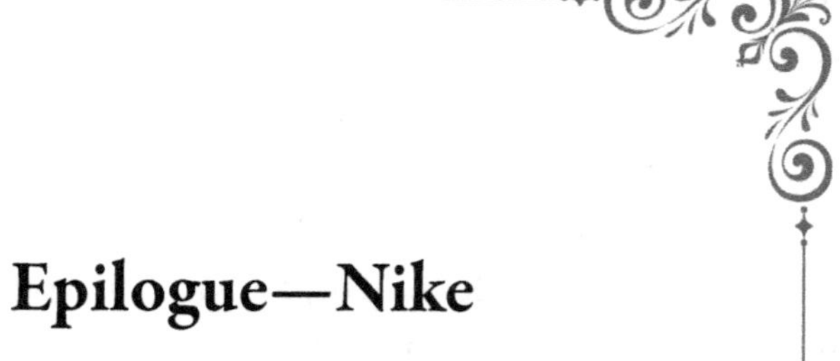

Epilogue—Nike

S*parklers*

Juggling bags of groceries, I kicked lightly on the bottom of the screen door to get Meri's attention. I could see her foraging through the cabinet. Her hair was in a short ponytail, and her clothing—well, my clothing—was mismatched with her shirt on backwards. At least she answered the door more quickly than she had yesterday when it had been raining and I couldn't find my key. I didn't realize she'd never heard a knock at the door before or even been inside a house until I stood banging on the door while she banged back. In typical Meri fashion, even the smallest thing turned out to be a fun game. At least for her. From the appearance of her heavily painted face in the window of the door, I could see she had discovered my small albeit expensive makeup stash. I'd have to show her how to apply eye makeup and lipstick without looking like a clown reject. For now I smiled and said, "Please open the door, Meri. Turn the handle to the right."

With a nod and a goofy grin, she rolled her eyes and did just that. At least she helped me bring in the groceries and put them away. She knew all about protecting the food. Meri loved human food. Once in a while, she'd come shake the dog food bag at me and frown miserably to remind me that she didn't appreciate my Top Dog food selection. I got the picture: if she was ever a dog again, I'd buy a different brand.

I hoped Heliope would help me integrate Meri into local human society, but so far no luck. Faydra's spell had sapped the goddess of her beauty, and it was all Heliope could do to keep it together. For example, I no longer needed an alarm clock to wake me up in the morning—I had Heliope weeping and wailing every time she woke up and looked in the mirror. I had no idea what to say to her except, "It will be okay—you're still beautiful." She didn't appreciate the platitudes, so I eventually gave up. Every morning she'd spend hours trying to cast a glamor spell on herself, but it always failed. That seemed to be part of Faydra's enchantment. Heliope sent a plea to the Order asking them to repeal the cruel spell. No word ever came; in fact, there were rumblings of major problems at the Secret Temple. I didn't ask for details. The less I knew, the better.

I poured a glass of soda and offered one to Meri. "Any calls from Heliope? She usually calls around lunch."

She shook her head sadly, looking as if she would cry at any moment. "It's not your fault, Meri. Don't blame yourself. Hey—want to help me pick out something for my date tonight?"

She put the glass down and raised her hands, signaling for me to wait. I laughed and agreed, taking a seat in the wooden kitchen chair as if I were about to view a fashion show. Heaven knew what I was about to see, but with Meri it would surely be a hoot. She came back modeling her first wardrobe suggestion, which was of course completely inappropriate: a skimpy purple lingerie top that I had forgotten about, paired with a pair of black spandex shorts.

"Um, too casual. Let's try something that doesn't show as much skin."

She stood with her hands on her hips and rolled her eyes dramatically.

"Trust me on this. What else you got?" She skipped off down the hall, and I sighed thinking about what my bedroom probably looked like. A minute or two later, she came back wearing a pink halter dress with polka-dot rain boots and a bright purple belt.

"That's better. Maybe the dress. Definitely not the boots. For a dress like that, open-toe shoes or maybe sandals." With a snap of her fingers, she bolted again, and I decided I needed to prepare lunch for us. We couldn't order french fries every day. I began washing lettuce and assorted vegetables for our lunch. Meri wasn't much of a vegetable person, but she'd have to make an effort.

Who was I kidding? I hated them too, but I wanted to look good for Ramara. I couldn't believe he'd asked me out, or I'd asked him. I couldn't remember now how it had all happened. But our first date was five hours away.

Five hours, twenty minutes and a few seconds. But who's counting?

I heard Meri slamming drawers, but I didn't yell at her. I had my friend back. It was really a miracle. Heliope had come through for me, even though her wonky magic had brought Meri back as a dog. At least she'd brought her back. To think, Heliope and I were actually friends now. How weird was that? I thought about calling her, but if she was busy with customers I'd just be a pain. When Heliope wasn't selling seashell keychains or some other tchotchkes to the rare fall tourists, she hawked her spells and potions to the island's supernaturate crowd. They politely thanked her and wisely never mentioned her current appearance. She was a natural saleswoman and could sell just about anything to anyone. Without the use of glamor magic.

She spent all her free time in the stock room of the souvenir shop trying to whip up a potion that would help her. She was obsessed with trying new concoctions, even wacky ones she found on the internet. I had to intervene a few times to make clear to her that radioactive material was illegal.

Despite the deeper lines and the gray hair, Heliope was still a beautiful woman, although she didn't believe it. Jolly sure thought so, but because of the smack to her pride, she rebuffed his every advance. Sometimes politely. "Stella needs to get her groove back first," as she put it to me.

She quoted movies all the time now, but at least she wasn't trying to cook—not lately, anyway. Between having one friend acting like an excited teenager and the other going through some kind of supernatural menopause, I was more than ready for my date. I smiled as Meri walked back in the room, still wearing the pink halter dress now with mismatched shoes and a bright orange head wrap. At least she had gotten the belt right. The thin brown leather belt was just the right touch.

I put the lettuce in the bowl and clapped my hands. "Meri, you did a great job! I love this and this. Let's get rid of those shoes and the head wrap. I think this is the outfit!" I hugged her as she bounced up and down happily. I wished she could speak to me, tell me what she thought about life here on land, but it wasn't to be. Mermaids never spoke, not in water or on land, but she was as always very expressive.

"Friend is so happy you are here, Meri. Friend missed you." She paused for a moment in my arms, stopped the bouncing and sighed deeply. She got very still and curled into my shoulder. I pulled back and said, "I never got a chance to thank you. Thank you, Meri, for saving my life."

She drew back and stared into my face. Her eyes were full of supernaturally luminous tears that slid down her cheeks. She wiped them away, staring at them and giving me a questioning look.

"It's okay. When your human heart feels certain emotions, it causes these—they call them tears. They will pass." She smiled at me and hugged me again. "All right, we've got to plan this date thing. I know it's going to be hard, but you have to hang out with Heliope this evening at the shop, okay? Jolly says he will come by and bring you both some ice cream." She looked at me questioningly and somehow I knew what she was asking. "No, you'll come home tonight, Meri. This *is* your home now. You'll only be gone for just a few hours." She clapped and spun around in circles.

Five hours later, Meri was leading me blindfolded outside and I was trying not to trip in my ridiculously high cork wedges. I rarely wore heels, but Ramara was tall so I thought I could pull it off. "Wait!" I said with a laugh. I stepped down the back stairs and could hear music playing softly in the kitchen window. I didn't know the song, but it sounded like a sweet country song about long-awaited love. Seemed appropriate.

Suddenly the blindfold was off and standing in front of me was Ramara, in a neat blue shirt and dressy blue jeans. He didn't bring flowers, but he had a bottle of expensive wine, which Meri took from him with a delighted smile. His hair was still damp and tucked behind his ears, and he looked nervous. It was sweet to see him so unsure of himself. That was a big change.

Meri had been busy while I took my shower and dressed. She'd strung my white Christmas tree lights all over the back porch and placed every candle I owned on my picnic table. The flames flickered in the breeze that blew up the hill from the shore below. The sun set in the distance. The air was cool, but I felt the blood rush to my face. We stood awkwardly facing one another for a few seconds. Meri zipped around the edge of the porch with a lighter. Somehow, some way, she'd managed to poke about two dozen sparklers in the sand and was busy lighting them. With all this light, I was afraid one of the offshore vessels would think the island was on fire. But it was the thought that counted.

It was a beautiful moment. Meri's lack of speech didn't stop her from gaping at us. She stomped her foot at me once while Heliope honked the horn in the driveway. She nudged me toward Ramara and with a silly wave left us alone.

"Hey there." I broke the silence first.

"Hey." His husky voice sounded quiet and careful. Then I realized that for the first time *ever* I could read Ramara's mind. It lasted only for a few seconds, but it was a revealing moment.

Maybe I should leave before she gets hurt?

I reached out and took his hands to reassure him. I would never confess that I'd accidentally invaded his mind. That was a secret worth keeping, and it might come in handy later. We were both in uncharted waters now. I tried not to stare at his arms, but I couldn't help myself. His tattoos were completely gone; the skin on his hands was perfectly smooth—even the battle scars had disappeared. The Order had stripped him of those and his immortality. And he'd lost all that for me.

"Shall we dance?" I said to him with a smile.

"I've never danced before," he said, laughing nervously.

"I've seen you handle a sword. That's kind of a dance." I swayed in his arms, refusing to take no as an answer.

He chuckled a bit. "I've always been pretty rough on weaponry. I'd hate to hurt you, princess."

"You've never seen me dance, have you? I think it's *you* who'd better worry about getting hurt. I mean, come on, you've heard me sing. Let's try it anyway, Ramara. And for the last time, my friends call me Nik."

He pulled me close, and we shuffled under the strings of white lights. The man on the radio crooned a love song:

> *The smile on your face lets me know that you need me.*
> *There's a truth in your eyes saying you'll never leave me.*
> *The touch of your hand says you'll catch me if ever I fall.*
> *You say it best when you say nothing at all.*

We were terrible dancers. Ramara moved like a robot and I stepped on his feet twice, but we laughed through our first dance. When the song ended, we stayed in place and danced through another one. The second time around was better, not because we'd improved our moves, but because I got to feel him in my arms. And because I knew, without reading his mind, that he was crazy about me.

When the music faded, he stopped his shuffling and stared down at me. "It's not too late to walk away, Thessalonike." He peered down at me cautiously.

"Oh, yes it is, Ramara. Way too late."

Without another word, he leaned down to me, and I was thankful for the first time that night that I had worn heels. His warm lips met mine, and we kissed again and again.

With a wide smile that reached his sexy eyes, he answered me. "I hate it when you're right."

M. L. Bullock's Book List

If you think you've missed one of my books, here is a comprehensive list of everything.☺ All books are available on Amazon Kindle, and as paper books. Some are available as audiobooks.

SEVEN SISTERS
#1 Seven Sisters
#2 Moonlight Falls on Seven Sisters
#3 Shadows Stir at Seven Sisters
#4 The Stars That Fell
#5 The Stars We Walked Upon
#6 The Sun Rises Over Seven Sisters
#7 Beyond Seven Sisters
Bonus Christmas at Seven Sisters
Bonus The Ghost on the Swing
#8 Silent Night, Haunted Night
#9 Haunted Halls of Rosegate Manor
#10 Terror at Mossy Oak
#11 Dark Angel of Selma
The Ultimate Seven Sisters Collection
Seven Sisters Collection Vol. 1
Seven Sisters Collection Vol. 2
Seven Sisters Collection Vol. 3
IDLEWOOD
#1 The Ghosts of Idlewood
#2 Dreams of Idlewood

#6 The Spiritus Mirror

#7 The Captain of Water Street

#8 Return to the Leaf Academy

#9 The Rising of Lucy Vallow

Bonus Horror Ever After (A Gulf Coast Paranormal Extra)

GULF COAST PARANORMAL SEASON THREE

#1 Tower of Darkness

#2 Haunted Molly

#3 Dead Children's Playground

#4 The Malaga Demon

#5 A Hanging at Barton

#6 The Outlaw Screamer

TWELVE TO MIDNIGHT

#1 Mary Twelves

#2 Pieces of Twelves

BRYNN LEEDS HAUNTING

#1 We Walk in Darkness

MORGAN'S ROCK

#1 The Haunting of Joanna Storm

#2 The Hall of Shadows

#3 The Ghost of Joanna Storm

The Haunting at Morgan's Rock Trilogy

QUEEN MUMMY

#1 Queen Mummy

RIVER RUN

#1 River Run

#2 Blood Run

#3 Witch Child

River Run Collection

SOUTHLAND

#1 Southland

#2 Southland: Legacy

Southland: The Complete Collection

THE DESERT QUEEN

#1 The Tale of Nefret

#2 The Falcon Rises

#3 The Kingdom of Nefertiti

#4 The Song of the Bee Eater

The Desert Queen Collection

LOST CAMELOT

#1 Guinevere Forever

#2 Guinevere Unconquered

#3 The Undead Queen of Camelot

Lost Camelot Trilogy

SHABBY HEARTS (A Romantic Comedy Series)

#1 A Touch of Shabby

#2 Shabbier By the Minute

#3 Shabby By Night

#4 Shabby All the Way

#5 Star Spangled Shabby

#6 A Shabby Wedding

Shabby Hearts Collection

MISCELLANEOUS

Ghosts on a Plane

Dead Is the Loneliest Place to Be

After Ella

Ghosts of the Atlantis

BY MONICA BULLOCK

Delivered Me From Evil

ROSE FALLS

#1 Rose Falls

#2 Rose Shadows

#3 Rose Rising

Rose Falls Collection

THE NIKE CHRONICLES
Blue Water
Blue Wake
Blue Tide
The Nike Chronicles

Don't miss out!

Visit the website below and you can sign up to receive emails whenever M.L. Bullock publishes a new book. There's no charge and no obligation.

https://books2read.com/r/B-A-CXMC-JRPDF

BOOKS2READ

Connecting independent readers to independent writers.

Did you love *Blue Tide*? Then you should read *A Cup of Shadows* by M.L. Bullock and A.E. Chewning!

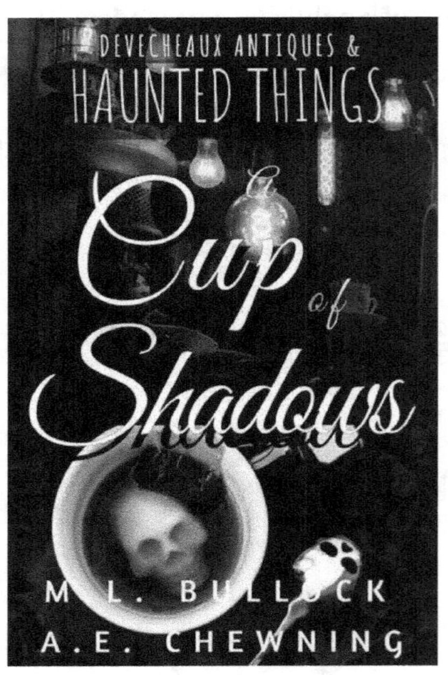

Henri and Detra Ann have poured their hearts into making their dream a reality--Devecheaux Antiques is open for business. But managing this kind of shop will require more than a business degree and a good eye for hard to find items. Haunted things have a nasty habit of making their way to this paranormal landmark. Trying to escape the shadows of the past, Detra Ann finds herself immersed in a paranormal investigation, but this time it's different. She can't run from the supernatural. Detra Ann must take a stand and allow the dead to speak.The Devecheauxs' new assistant, Mary Agnes Kelly--she prefers Aggie, is the one that's hiding secrets. When a curious object in the shop goes missing, Aggie's abilities are exposed and she is thrust into a world of vengeance, murder and the afterlife. The college student will have to muster all her courage to face down the ghosts of Devecheaux

Antiques--and her own demons.Opening the door to the paranormal, Aggie comes face to face with a spirit close to Detra Ann's heart, leading them both to reveal what happened in the past and help the unhappy ghost rest in peace.Will Detra Ann and Aggie be able to expose the truth or will all be lost in the shadows of history?Find out in A Cup of Shadows by authors M.L. Bullock and A.E. Chewning. A Cup of Shadows in Book One in their new series Devecheaux Antiques and Haunted Things. If you love Seven Sisters, Idlewood and Haunted Gracefield, you'll enjoy reading A Cup of Shadows.

Also by M.L. Bullock

Create and Prosper
The Prolific Writer: How to Write and Create a Successful Catalog of Books

Delta Hex
The Devil's Bayou

Desert Queen Saga
The Tale of Nefret
The Falcon Rises
The Kingdom of Nefertiti
The Song of the Bee Eater

Devecheaux Antiques and Haunted Things
The Ghost Mirror
The Darkening Door

Devecheaux Antiques and Haunted Things Trilogy Series
Devecheaux Antiques and Haunted Things
A Cup of Shadows
A Voice From Her Past
A Watch Of Weeping Angels

Gulf Coast Paranormal
The Ghosts of Kali Oka Road
The Ghosts of the Crescent Theater
A Haunting on Bloodgood Row
The Legend of the Ghost Queen
A Haunting at Dixie House
The Ghost Lights of Forrest Field
The Ghost of Gabrielle Bonet
The Ghost of Harrington Farm
The Creature on Crenshaw Road
A Ghostly Ride in Gulfport
The Ghosts of Phoenix No.7
The Maelstrom of the Leaf Academy
The Ghosts of Oakleigh House
The Spirits of Brady Hall
The Gray Lady of Wilmer

Gulf Coast Paranormal Season Three
Tower of Darkness
Haunted Molly
Dead Children's Playground

Gulf Coast Paranormal Season Two
The Wayland Manor Haunting
The Beast of Limerick House
The Beast of Limerick House
A Haunting at Goliath Cave
Death Among the Roses
The Captain of Water Street
Return to the Leaf Academy

Gulf Coast Paranormal Trilogy Series
Ghosted
Haunted
Dead
Spooked
Paranormal

Haunting Passions
For the Love of Shadows
Her Haunted Heart

Idlewood
The Ghosts of Idlewood
Dreams of Idlewood
The Whispering Saint
The Haunted Child

Laurel House
Whispers

Lost Camelot
Guinevere Unconquered
The Undead Queen of Camelot

Lost Camelot Trilogy
Guinevere Forever

Marietta
The Bones of Marietta
Footsteps of Angels

Morgans Rock
The Haunting of Joanna Storm
The Hall of Shadows
The Ghost of Joanna Storm

Nike Augustine
Blue Water
Blue Wake
Blue Tide

Return to Seven Sisters
The Roses of Mobile
All the Summer Roses
Blooms Torn Asunder
A Garden of Thorns
Wreath of Roses

River Run
River Run

Rose Falls
Rose Falls
Rose Shadows
Rose Rising

Scary Fall Stories
Horrible Little Things

Seven Sisters
Seven Sisters
Moonlight Falls On Seven Sisters
Shadows Stir At Seven Sisters
The Stars That Fell
The Stars We Walked Upon

The Sun Rises Over Seven Sisters
Beyond Seven Sister
Ghost on a Swing

Shabby Hearts
A Touch Of Shabby
Shabbier By The Minute
Shabby By Night
Shabby All The Way
Star Spangled Shabby
A Shabby Wedding

Southern Gothic
Being With Beau
Death's Last Darling
Spook House

Southland
Southland

Sugar Hill
Wife Of The Left Hand
Fire On The Ramparts
Blood By Candlelight
The Starlight Ball
His Lovely Garden

Summerleigh
The Belles of Desire, Mississippi
The Ghost Of Jeoprady Belle
The Lady In White
Loxley Belle

Supernatural Support Group
Circle of Shadows

The Mummy Queen's Revenge
Queen Mummy

The Vampires of Rock and Roll
Elegant Black
Elegant Death

Twelve to Midnight
Mary Twelves

Standalone
The Hauntings of Idlewood
Lost Camelot
The Desert Queen Collection

Haunting Passions
Ghosts on a Plane
Halloween Screams
Dead Is the Loneliest Place to Be
Ghost Story
Believer's Guide to Paranormal Ministry
Haunted Chronicles of the Leaf Academy
Haunting Paranormal
Falls the Shadow
The Mourning Heart
Marietta

Watch for more at www.mlbullock.com.

About the Author

Author M.L. Bullock enjoys the laid-back atmosphere and the spooky vibe of the Gulf Coast, especially the region's historic districts and sites. When she isn't visiting her favorite haunts in New Orleans or Old Mobile, you can find her flipping through old photographs or newspaper clippings in search of new inspiration.

Read more at www.mlbullock.com.